Blue Turquoise

Cynthia Vannoy

Blue Turquoise   Vannoy

First Edition
Copyright   Cynthia Vannoy, 2015
All Rights Reserved

Vannoy, Cynthia
Fiction, paranormal romace, Wyoming

ISBN-13: 978-0692416341

 **Back Hills Press**
Clearmont, Wyo

Chapter 1
Present

The old buildings of the deserted town loomed over the road, the late summer sun creating dark shadows in the empty doors and glass-less windows. The windows looking like empty eye sockets in wooden skulls.

It was quiet along the twisting red-shale road, Jenny hadn't seen a single car on the ten mile drive from Crystal Creek. An old train-track looked abandoned, with weeds growing though the ties and along the rails.

It would be dark soon. Jenny took the lens cap off her digital camera and began snapping some photos. Wild Rose, Wyoming. Or, Wyoming Territory when Wild Rose was a town, the town where he great-great-grandfather, Barney Morgan, was once a sheriff and a judge.

There were three of the old buildings still standing, including the ruins of an old false-fronted building that could have been a saloon or a general store.   Several crumbling foundations were scattered about, one with a set of steps that went up into nothingness.

A few photos would suffice, Jenny thought, and she hoped she could find an old map or at least a description of the town in the library in Red Bluffs. The sun had dropped behind the mountains, and the shadows from the buildings were long on the ground.

She took several photos, and walked around the ruins, wondering what the town had looked like in it's heyday, wondering if she could find any old photos of it to add to the book.

She was stooping down to get a shot showing the largest building silhouetted against the evening sky when a rough voice yelled, "Hey".

Jenny jumped. When she parked her Explorer minutes before, the road and prairie had completely deserted. She had crawled through a barb-wire fence, at the risk of her jeans and shirt, but she didn't think anyone would mind.

She hadn't heard the sound of anyone approaching. She spun around and came nose to white-snipped* nose with a tall, long-legged black horse. Looking way up, she saw the rider, black

(*a short white strip on a horse's nose.)

cowboy hat shielding his eyes, and a grim mouth. He looked at her in silence. She began to wonder if he were real, or a ghost, or a figment of her imagination. He was less out of place on this desolate prairie than herself and her Ford Explorer parked on the gravel road.

"You're trespassing, you know." The man's voice sounded young, and Jenny noticed the hair curling out from under his hat was a dark chocolate brown. His face was shadowed under his hat, but she could see his square, strong chin, shadowed a little with dark whiskers.

"I didn't think anyone would mind if I slipped through the fence and took a couple of photographs. There weren't any signs posted."

"There are at the gates," the cowboy said. "Most people don't go across fences out here. What are you taking photos of?"

"I need some of this ghost town. It

used be the town of Wild Rose." Jenny lifted her chin, wondering what argument she could muster to convince this cowboy that she wasn't hurting anything.

He grinned suddenly. "If you want photos of this ruin, feel free. But just don't go wondering too far out in the pasture. This is private land, and, beside that, these ruins are great hiding places for rattlesnakes. Have fun."

With that, he turned his horse's head, touched the black with a spur, and trotted off.

Jenny watched him, as he grew smaller in the distance of the grassy plain, when he suddenly dropped out of sight. Vanished. She began to wonder if he had really been there, talking to her, or if he had been a figment of her imagination, which had always been pretty good.

Her eyes swept the desolate prairie, hoping he would reappear, but there was nothing there. No deer, no cattle, no sign of life at all. She shivered slightly, although the day was warm. Spooky out here, nothing but grass and endless rolling hills and valleys. And possibly rattlesnakes. She wished the cowboy hadn't mentioned them. Well, she had enough photos anyway, and it was getting dark.

She put the lens cap back on the camera and turned back towards her Explorer. She would be glad to get back to Billings, and the bustle of the medium-sized city.

Back at the Explorer, she settled herself in the seat and turned the key. Nothing happened. She tried again, and still nothing. "Oh, great," She thought. "Now what?"

It was a long ways to anywhere. Walking didn't seem to be an option. She hoped someone would come along, but the road ahead and behind her was empty. Totally empty. Obviously the residents didn't travel this back road at night. Even if someone came along, her survival instinct said that getting into a stranger's car at night was not a good idea.

She looked at her disabled vehicle. There was no sense looking under the hood, she knew how to check the oil and the antifreeze and washer fluid, and that was it. If a belt had broken, she had nothing to repair it with anyway.

She stamped her foot in frustration. Maybe the cowboy was a jinx. He had somehow jinxed her car.

She had two choices. Wait out the night in the Explorer, or walk back to Crystal Creek, where, she was sure, nothing would be open anyway. The town, like many small western towns, rolled up the sidewalks after dark.

The old buildings towering over the road had no answers, nor did her silent car, looking out of place among the old buildings.

Jenny felt there should be horses and wagons, and a worn dirt track, full of tumbleweeds.

In fact, ever since she had turned off I-25 unto the secondary road to Crystal Creek and the red shale one to Wild Rose, it had felt like a trip back to the past. After two exhausting days of research at the Wyoming State Archives in Cheyenne, her mind had been firmly set in the 1800s. Now, stranded in the old ghost town, looking out over the dark hills, she almost expected to see a line of Indians on the skyline, or hear the snort of a horse or the sound of a gunfight.

Looking at the long, dark shale road, it was really dark without the street lights she was accustom to in town, she decided against walking. She had seen no houses along the road, there wasn't a sign of human habitation anywhere.

She found a flashlight in the glove box, and for a wonder the batteries weren't dead. She got out of the car, walked around to the back of the Explorer to see if she had left any winter clothing in the back end.

She found a dusty old coat to help keep out the night chill, and half a case of Dasani water. She thanked her habit, often derided by her mother, of not cleaning out her vehicle on a regular basis. The coat had been there for months, maybe years. The water since the camping trip with girl friends last summer.

Inside the car she found a bruised apple, a box of crackers and a couple packages of string cheese. Not exactly what she had planned on for supper, but it would at least fill her stomach to some extent.

Slightly cheered by the fact that she had warmth, food and drink, Jenny crawled back into the front seat of the Explorer, snuggled up inside the coat, nibbled on the crackers and prepared to wait out the night. It would be a long wait. Her glow-in-the dark watch said 9:15. She had hoped to be in Red Bluffs tonight, and thought longingly of a motel room, a shower and a soft bed.

She tried the key once more, but the same grinding sound came from under the hood. There was no way the car was going to start.

There was a glow on the eastern horizon, and within a few minutes the half-moon emerged over the hills, adding some light to dark landscape. The old buildings stood out against the hills, the moonlight reflected off the false fronts but leaving the empty windows blank and dark, like the eyes of a skull. Shivering, even though the coat was warm, Jenny turned her back on the empty buildings and tried not the think of the term 'ghost town.'

It was sad, the once bustling, living town reduced to an empty skeleton. Eerie stories kept surfacing in her mind. Phantom cowboys, ghosts guarding old houses and mine shafts, lights where no lights should be, strange sounds.

She remembered a painting she had once seem in an art gallery in Jackson, Wyoming. A phantom stage coach reflected in the broken window of an old saloon. She wished she had broke down anywhere but here.

Keeping her back to the skeletal buildings, she burrowed into the coat, and tried to sleep. The smell of wild roses drifted thought the partway open window.

Chapter 2
1885

The music seemed to come from the
deserted town site. Sitting up, Jenny
wondered if a car had driven up without
her hearing it. But the music sounded
different, somehow, than modern music.

The moon was riding high now, but
it wasn't the moon making the soft,
yellow light that seemed to flow into the
car. Jenny blinked her eyes, but the light
was still there. It was coming from the
windows of a house Jenny hadn't seen
earlier. The music, too, was tinny

sounding, and faint. It sounded like an old, out of tune, piano.

Jenny looked around her, and gasped in amazement. She was in the middle of town. Not the ghost town, but a real town. There were lights in the windows of the houses, not harsh electric light, but soft yellow glow.

The largest building had the most windows, and was brightly lit. It also seemed to be the source of the music. There were four horses standing in front, tied to the hitching rail, saddled and hip shot.* A wagon stood empty in the street.

"Why didn't I notice that before?" Jenny wondered aloud.

She opened the Explorer door, got out and walked towards the music. The air smelled of wild roses but also of dust and horse manure. As she got closer to the building, she could smell pipe and

(*when a horse stands resting a hind foot)

16

cigarette smoke and stale whiskey. Normally, she would been reluctant to enter a bar this time of night, but maybe there would be someone there who could start her car.

She tripped over something, and almost fell. For some reason she couldn't take her usual long, free stride. It felt as if she were hobbled. Looking down, she saw she was wearing, not her jeans, but a long skirt. That was strange, she thought, adjusting her stride.

The door to the saloon was not the traditional bat-wings, but a solid wood door that was propped open with a boot to let in the night air. A rough looking man opened the door wider and strode out. He saw Jenny, and tipped his limp-brimmed cowboy hat.

"Evenin' Mz Jen," he said politely, stepping back and holding the door open for her. Jenny nodded to him, wondering who he was and why he knew her name.

Inside, the saloon was hardly impressive. The most eye-catching feature was a large mirror that dominated the wall behind the bar. The bartender, a lean, fox-faced man wearing a dingy gray apron, was wiping glasses behind the bar and looked up as she carefully climbed up on a rough wooden stool.

"Evenin' Miz Jen. Your usual?"

Jenny nodded, not knowing what her usual was, but she hoped it was something she liked. She wondered again why everyone seemed to know her. She looked around, and saw the music was coming from an old-fashioned piano in one corner. A man with a black handle-bar mustache was playing it.

The bartender returned, bearing a glass which, upon a careful taste, revealed itself to be a weak whiskey and water. Jenny seldom drank, and usually drank sweet wine. The whiskey tasted smokey and burned her throat as she sipped it.

She glanced around, feeling out of the talk that waved and undulated, buzzing like so many insect voices, as annoying as the cigarette smoke that drifted over and stung her eyes. The bar was rough plank, and she snagged the arm of her dress as she reached for her drink.

She looked at the calendar behind the bar with a huge picture of a cowboy roping a longhorn steer, the month was June, but the year was 1885.

For some reason this didn't seem strange.

Jenny took another drink of the whiskey, feeling the slightly buzzed feeling as the alcohol swam through her blood. No paid her any mind, except for the bartender, who kept a watch on the level of her drink, ready to refill it if necessary.

She turned around on the stool to

see the other occupants of the bar. There were rough cowboys, one wearing spurs with huge Mexican rowels that clinked as he swirled his partner, looking very much the part of her profession, in a merry dance to the music from the piano. Those who felt lucky were at a nearby table, slapping cards down with deadly seriousness.

She sensed an expectancy in the air, a feeling of waiting. Jenny felt as if it had something to do with her, she felt as if she were waiting for someone, but she didn't know who. The bartender filled her drink again, but didn't engage her in conversation. She was glad of that, as she didn't know what to say anyway. Between the whiskey and the strangeness of it all, she was feeling pleasantly dizzy and relaxed.

Suddenly, a blast of cold air on the back of her neck broke the spell, and the tension in the room was almost tangible.

She knew, without knowing how she knew, that whoever was standing behind her in the doorway was the person that she had been waiting for.

"Wolf. He's back in town," the bartender said, more of a mutter to himself than to Jenny. The very name sent a shiver down Jenny's spine.

She turned around slowly, having to crane her neck to see who caused such a chill feeling in the room.

The man standing in the doorway was tall and lean. He had wide shoulders, covered by a brown shirt. His hair, under the wide-brimmed cowboy hat, was black, and hung long and straight to below his shoulders.

Of all the details, Jenny was most aware of his eyes. Dark brown eyes, fastened on hers, compelling her not to look away.

The man walked up to the bar, and the bartender set a glass and a bottle in front of him, then edged away, as one might move away from a poisonous snake, slowly, so as not to provoke a strike. The piano picked up the tempo again, and the dancers dipped and swayed, still Jenny had a feeling that the patrons were watching Wolf out of the corner of their eyes, as one might watch an unpredictable lion or bad-tempered bull.

Wolf took the glass of whiskey and downed it in one long swallow, then poured another out of the bottle, and offered it to Jen. She shook her head. "I've, I've had enough."

Wolf nodded, and poured another drink for himself. "I don't have long, Jen. Let's go." He put a silver dollar and a two dimes on the bar, and moved aside to let Jenny take the lead. Somehow, she knew where to go.

Chapter 3
1885

Outside, the street was dark, many of the homeowners had now blown out their lights, the windows were black. A horse nickered at the hitch rail, and somewhere an insane rooster crowed at the nearly full moon.

The house Jen stopped at was small. Beside the door the moonlight caught a small patch of flowers, and as Jenny's skirt brushed against the rose bush near the door, the sweet scent of roses filled the air.

She pushed the door open, letting in the moonlight that barely illuminated the small kitchen. Jen could make out a table with a hurricane oil lamp sitting in the middle; two chairs; and a large Majestic coal stove crouching in the corner like a sleeping bear.

Wolf took a match from his shirt pocket, struck it, removed the lamp's chimney, turned up the wick, and lit the oil lamp. A warm glow lit the room, and objects no longer looked shadowed, but solid and real. Scattered on the table like fall leaves were several sheets of paper, with names, rough sketches, and reward monies posted on them.

Wolf saw her glance at the papers. "I came here first, Jen," he said, taking her in his arms.

"And I wasn't here," Jen said, feeling bad for him but feeling safe and warm in his arms, with her head nestled against his shoulder.

"You're here now," Wolf said. "God, its good to hold you. That trail gets cold and lonely, and even the campfire can't warm me. But I always come back, Jen. No matter how long the trail is, I'll always come back. I almost have enough money to re-stock the ranch. And I'm getting closer to him. Then I'll quit this god-awful business and settle down to raising stock and a passel of kids. We'll find a preacher and make it legal. Then we can build something."

Jen reached up and touched his face, running her fingers along the rough stubble on his chin. "I don't need a preacher. I just want to be with you, whether its legal or not. I can stand the whispers around town, and the snubs by the 'ladies'. What I can't stand are the long, lonely nights without you, wondering if you're laying somewhere dead or dying, and I'm not there to help you. Its a dangerous job, Wolf." She didn't say any more, she had said it all before. Many times. She had pleaded. "Give it up. Please. You have the land, you proved up years ago. Let's go there. We can rebuild, buy some cattle. Whatever you have is enough."

She had said that before, but it hadn't worked.

Wolf's face turned cold. His brown eyes, warm when they looked at her, were as cold as rocks under a frozen stream. "I'm dangerous too. I have no intention of dying before I get Arizona. Just one last man, and then I'll quit. I swear, Jen."

"Why?" Jenny asked. "Why do you have this obsession with him. He's who you want, not the money. If it were just money, you could get that somewhere else." Somewhere safer, she wanted to add, but didn't. "What did that man do to you that you can't rest until you find him?"

She was still nestled in his arms, but she could feel the coldness, and the stiffness in his body.

"It was a long time ago. An old score." His voice was chill. "One day I'll bring him in across the saddle."

Jen loved him, but sometimes, like now, it seemed that her love was the same one might have for a caged but still savage wolf, and that she was the only one who could tame him and fondle him. Still, this hatred he had for Jesse Arizona frightened her.

Arizona was the leader of a crew of outlaws who robbed stages and banks and fancied themselves the Wyoming equivalent of the James Gang of Missouri, ruthless, no-account killer, who robbed and killed throughout the territory, and frequently robbed the Cheyenne-Deadwood stages, until they owners began putting extra guards on board. Then they turned their attention to the local mail stages, especially when they were carrying payrolls or gold from the Deadwood mines.

Wolf had been trailing him for three years, just before Jen had met him and fell in love.

During that time Arizona had eluded capture. It seemed as if he had special protection from either God or Satan. Every time Wolf mentioned Arizona, Jen could see the deep hatred smoldering behind his eyes.

Wolf never talked of his past, and Jen had learned never to ask.

"I'm sorry," Jen said, nuzzling his neck, knowing she had to apologize. "I didn't mean to bring it up. It's just that it makes you so bitter. So full of hate. You used to bring them in for trial, now you bring most of them in across your saddle. Is it necessary, or is it just quicker?"

He pushed her from him, so

roughly that she staggered against the table, rapping her elbow painfully and joggling the lamp.

"I suppose you would rather see me dead instead?" His tone was sarcastic. "The last three thought they were good, but luckily for me, they weren't good enough."

"Sorry," Jen said again, nursing her bruised elbow. "I didn't know."

Sometimes she wondered if loving him were worth it. Worth the long, lonely nights, and the sly looks from the towns people. Wolf always promised to give up his dangerous work, but after three years he was deeper into the bounty hunting than ever. Jen was beginning to think that he enjoyed the hunt, and the kill at the end.

"Well, now you know," Wolf said, then his mood changed and he reached for her again, pulling her back into his arms. "Ah, hell Jen. I'm sorry. It's been a

long, cold trail. I want to come home to
your loving, not your disapproval. I hate
this job, but right now I have to do it, for
myself and for someone else. Someday
I'll tell you about it, but just believe me
when I say I have to do it. Trust me, Jen."

Jen nodded wearily. It felt warm in
his arms, her head nestled against his
broad chest. His shirt smelled of
campfire smoke, horses and sweat. "I just
get so damn lonely. I want to strike out at
whoever is keeping us apart," Jen said.

"Here," Wolf said, moving away
from her and reaching into the pocket of
his shirt. "I picked this up off an old
Navaho gal down south. Thought you
might like it."

He held out a length of turquoise
stones, strung together on a length of
buckskin. The necklace seemed to glow
with a blue radiance, and Jen took it
gingerly, feeling the smooth, waxy texture
of the stones.

At the apex of the necklace was a piece of antler, carved in the shape of a howling wolf. The stones felt cool to the touch, not warm as they should have been, having been in Wolf's pocket. She wondered if they would feel cold against her skin.

"Its beautiful," she said, "Thank you."

"The Indians say turquoise brings good luck, that a spirit lives inside the stones. The wolf is a protector of the Indians, and his spirit lives inside the fetish stone. The wolf is my spirit as well. This way, I am always with you. Let me put it on." Wolf said, taking the necklace from Jen's hands and slipped it over her head.

His hands stroked the curve of her neck, and fingered with the pins that held her hair up in the respectable knot behind her head. Jen leaned against him as she felt the hair cascade down her

31

shoulders and back.

Wolf's hands touched hers, then moved lower, gently working the buttons and sliding the dress off her shoulders.

Jen felt the cool air on her bare shoulders, and the cold feel of the turquoise stones against her skin. Reaching up, she put her arms around Wolf's neck.

Chapter 4
Present

Jenny Morgan woke with a start, wondering what there was about the ghost town that produced such a vivid dream.

The ghost town looked different in the golden light of early morning. The building that last night been a saloon, filled with laughing, dancing men and brightly dressed women, was now simply a stark, ruined shape against the sky. The other buildings still standing were windowless, roofless, looking one step away from collapse.

There were no more than three houses standing now, and Jenny wondered how her mind had conjured up and entire town based on those few ruined buildings.

She remembered the smells, the smoke in the saloon, Wolf's scent, of horses and homespun; and even the bitter taste of whiskey, still foul in her mouth. That was weird. She had never even tasted whiskey before, yet the sharp, smokey taste still lingered.

A drink of water was in order. She twisted the top off the plastic water bottle and took a swallow, still thinking of the dream. How real it had seemed. She shook her head. "I must have one heck of imagination."

Consciously, she knew the dream had been the result of her overactive imagination, the eerie deserted town, and the cowboy she had met briefly yesterday.

Dreams were dreams, products of the sleeping mind trying to make sense of the events of the previous day before filing them in memory slots. Rather, Jenny thought, like a mess of files awaiting the appropriate slots in a large filing cabinet.

She took another sip of the water. It didn't do anything to fill her empty stomach. She longed for a cup of hot coffee, and a cinnamon roll. With cream cheese frosting. Her stomach rumbled at the thought.

She tried the key again, but the starter ground dully. At least she could walk in the daylight without stumbling over something and breaking a leg. The sun was just peeking over the eastern horizon, and her watch said 5:45.

It was a beautiful morning, with the sun sending golden rays across the green irrigated hay fields. The air smelled of grass and alfalfa hay, but not wild roses. Strange. Nor did Jenny see any roses blooming nearby. She did see a few straggling bushes growing near an old foundation, with a few crumpled pink flowers, but not nearly enough to scent the air.

It was still cool; her jacket felt good. Jenny couldn't remember how far she had driven last night, but she hoped it wouldn't be too long a walk. She picked up her purse and camera bag off the seat, and stepped out of the vehicle. As she turned to lock the door, she saw something blue in the dust beside her foot.

Jenny felt a chill run down her spine as she picked up the turquoise necklace. She fingered the lumpy stones and the tiny howling wolf. The necklace was intact, and the stones were smooth without chips or nicks.

Someone must have lost it, Jenny thought. But it was strange that it had appeared in her dream. Maybe the dream had been telling her she would find such a necklace. When she got back to town, she would look in the paper lost and found and see if she could track down the owner. To make sure she didn't lose it, she slipped the necklace over her head, and tucked in under her shirt. The stones felt cool and smooth on her chest.

The town looked different in the early light, so she took some more photos before beginning what could be a long walk back to Crystal Creek, or at least to where she could get cell service.

She was walking briskly along the road, actually enjoying the bright morning. At any other time the sound of a car engine would have been an annoying interruption, but looking at the long road ahead, Jenny was just hopeful whoever was driving would stop for her.

She wasn't as worried in the light of day about accepting a ride.

A maroon Chevy pickup drove up beside her, and the driver slowed to a stop. Jenny walked over to the driver's side of the pickup, and wasn't too surprised to see that her rescuer was the cowboy who accused her of trespassing yesterday.

"Need help?" he asked.

Jenny could only stare for a moment, while the conscious part of her mind urged her to quickly take advantage of his offer. It was weird, though. Not only did she recognize him from yesterday morning, but he could have been a twin to Wolf, the bounty hunter that played a prominent part in her dream. Wolf, even to silver band on his black cowboy hat.

He was looking at her strangely. "You okay?"

Jenny shook her head.

"My, my car broke down. It won't start. I spent the night there," she gestured back towards the ruined town.

And I had a weird dream, and you were in it, and I'm upset, her subconscious mind added.

The man looked at her with an even stranger expression Jenny wondered if she had spoken the dream aloud. The man snapped his fingers. "You're that photographer I talked to yesterday."

Jenny nodded, still confused by the resemblance.

"You said spent the night here?" he glanced at the ghost town, a little uneasily, Jenny thought. "Good thing you're not a local. People say this place is haunted," the man grinned.

As if I didn't know, Jenny thought. Aloud, she said, "Haunted or not, I didn't have much choice. I sure didn't want to take off walking in the dark and break a leg or something." Jenny felt a little better. This wasn't her dream man, but a modern day rancher, out on some early errand.

She didn't really believe in ghosts, or haunted houses. Her experience was a figment of her own imagination, coupled with the atmosphere of the old ghost town.

"I can take a look at your car, if you want," the cowboy said. "Maybe I can get it going for you. Hop in."

"Its not far back, I'll walk," Jen said.

The man drove his pickup next to her Explorer, and jumped out. He lifted the hood in one smooth movement. He jiggled some wires, and using a handkerchief from his pocket he wiped the battery terminals.

"Go ahead, try to start it," he instructed Jenny. She did, and nothing happened. Just a click. Walking back to the tool box in the back of his pickup, the man produced a set of jumper cables and after some jiggling with his pickup hood, attached them to the batteries.

"Try it again."

There was nothing but another click.

The man pulled his head out from under the hood and dropped it shut. "Might be your starter. I can call a tow truck when I get back in cell service, might take them two hours to get here, or I can give you a ride to town and you can call one. I was heading into Red Bluffs for horse feed anyway."

Jenny thought about hot coffee, and breakfast. Her stomach felt empty as a paper sack.

"I'll take the lift, with thanks." she said, re-locking the car and shrugging her purse on her shoulder, swinging her long brown hair out of the way of the strap.

"No problem," the man said, even opening the passenger side door for

Jenny, such a burst of chivalry surprised her, and she smiled at him. He grinned back, waited until she was safely inside, then carefully shut the door, and went around to the driver's side. As he walked in front of the pickup, Jenny noticed his wide shoulders and narrow hips. A well built cowboy, she thought. She was still getting the double-image impression, bounty-hunter Wolf and Mr. Cowboy.

The pickup smelled like horses and leather, and in the back seat was an elaborately tooled saddle and a well-used saddle blanket.

He jumped in behind the wheel, and said, "My name is Rand Logan. I live back up there," his arm made a sweeping gesture towards the north. "What brings you to this neck of the woods, since you're from Montana, or maybe even farther afield."

"I'm Jenny Morgan, and I live in Billing actually. I'm writing a book for the Wyoming Historical Society about my great-great-grandfather, Barney Morgan. He lived in Wild Rose back in 1885 and '86"

Rand grinned. "So one day I'll be saying, 'I knew that author. Even rescued her one day and helped her to get her Explorer going.' Maybe I should get an autograph now before you get famous."

Jenny laughed at his teasing. "Maybe. But this might be a one-time thing. I'm actually a school librarian by profession. That's why I can take the summer off to do the research and write the book on weekends and holidays."

The drive to Red Bluffs was more scenic along the back road that it was along the paved highway. They topped one hill and the view of the Big Horn Mountains, warm with morning sun, make Jenny gasp in appreciation. "Wow, what a view," she said.

Rand smiled. "I prefer this road to

the highway. Shorter and a lot more scenic."

"You said your great-great-grandfather was Barney Morgan? On one part of our land we have the Morgan pasture, and what we call the Morgan homestead. I wonder if there is a connection?"

"He did homestead around here. If it is his, I would like to look at it someday."

"No problem. But call Henry Frost. If you've got a pen I'll give you the number. The homestead is on our land, but access is easier from his place."

She wrote down the number. "Thanks. That would be great," she told him.

Rand proved to be an interesting companion, pointing out interesting features of the landscape, "We call that Eagle Rock," he said, pointing to an upright rock sticking out of a hill. It did look like an eagle from a certain angle. He told her of Indian chiefs and outlaws that once roamed the now settled lands.

Jenny tried to remember the name of the outlaw in her dream, but in the way of all dreams it was already fading, and she couldn't remember who he was.

Besides, she wasn't sure she wanted to tell anyone about her experience in the ghost town just yet, especially if it was rumored to be haunted.

"You said the locals felt the ruins of Wild Rose were haunted, what kind of stories do they tell about it?"

Rand grinned, and looked off into the distance, down the winding red shale road ahead of them. Jenny could feel a ghost story coming on. She wasn't sure if she really wanted to hear it.

"Several things have been seen and heard," Rand said. "The town was abandoned in 1892, after the railroad opted for a shorter route, and was relocated and the name was changed to Crystal Creek. Many of the houses from Wild Rose were moved to the new town site. People who lived in those houses would hear footsteps on the wooden floors, and hear voices when no one was around. In one house a bloodstain would appear on the kitchen floor every year. It was discovered that a railroad worker had killed his girlfriend there during a fight."

Rand shook his head. "Strange things happen in this world. In the town site, what's left of it, people often say they see lights in the windows and hear music. But, seeings as most of the people who tell these stories have been at one of the local watering holes, their stories have been discounted."

He shrugged. "When I was in school, the kids would dare each other to spend a night there, but as far as I know, no one ever did."

He glanced at Jenny. "I didn't

know I was such a good story teller. You look like you <u>have</u> seen a ghost."

Chapter 5
Present

Jenny didn't dare tell him about her experience, but now she felt frightened. Writing it off as just a dream had been easy, but maybe it hadn't been. Maybe there really were spirits there, and she had seen them. That was something she had to think about before she told anyone.

"Are the haunted houses still in Crystal Creek?" Jenny asked.

"Many are. Occasionally someone rents one, but usually they're vacant. Not to many people like living with spooks."

Jenny laughed, but she felt goosebumps on her arm.

They traveled in silence for a time, then Jenny said, "You've lived here all your life?"

"Yep. My great-great-grandfather homesteaded here, then my grandfather expanded on the property, buying up some of his neighbors. My Dad took over when Grandpop retired, and he added some more acreage. I plan to keep it going. The original land has been in the Logan family for over 100 years."

There was pride in his voice. Justifiable, Jenny thought. So many family ranches were being sold off, taken over by urban sprawl or purchased by rich corporations. It was rare to find a ranching family that had survived the years of drought, high interest loans, and ofter low cattle markets.

"What do you raise," she asked, fascinated.

"Longhorn cattle. Registered show stock, low birth weight bulls and roping stock." He grinned. "Grandpop would have been proud. He raised Longhorns as well, but we expanded on them and added registered cattle. One of my heifers won grand champion in state and reserve champion at the Denver Stock Show last year."

He slowed down to let a fawn deer and her mother cross the road ahead of them.

"Next year I intend to sweep the boards at Denver. I bought the Champion Heifer. Never did tell Pa what she cost."

Jenny was impressed. The National Western Stock Show held in Denver, Colorado each winter, was one of the biggest livestock shows in the nation.

"Tell me about your book," Rand said, after a pause of several miles.

"Barney Morgan, my great-great-grandfather, was a sheriff, then a judge, and later was a senator in the early days of Wyoming's statehood. The Wyoming Historical Society is doing a series on the early pioneers, and he was one they wanted a book on. Being related to him, I was asked to write it. "

"Sounds kind of boring," Rand said.

"Actually, it isn't. He actually lobbied for woman's suffrage. He seemed to be very much for woman's liberation, which was unusual back then. Especially since when he was young he was a real hell-raiser, or at least that what my research so far shows. If the homestead on your place was his, that would be a good thing to add to the book. Funny, too, his grandfather was a sheriff, and another ancestor was a judge."

Rand nodded.   "Do you know when your great-great-grandfather sold his homestead? Kind of funny if he did sell to my family."

"Interesting," Jenny admitted, making a mental note to see if she could find out that information.

"A lot of homesteaders starved out, mainly in the 20s and 30s. Depression time. But, from what you're telling me, Morgan probably didn't go broke. He must have sold out and just moved out of the area."

"That could be," Jenny said. "But your granddad must have had money, to buy out his neighbors."

"Grandpop did say once that his father kept his credit good, so maybe it was more that than being rich. I don't know. He did manage to hang on, not sure how," Rand said. "

Jenny wanted to ask Rand what his

great-great-grandfather's name was, but didn't want to tell him why she wondered. She was still confused and disturbed by the eerie resemblance between Wolf and Rand Logan. She wondered if Wolf had been real, and, if so, if he was related to Rand.

"No one has ever traced our family tree," Rand said, as if reading her thoughts. "Just as far back as the great-great-grandparents. Mom makes a stab at it now and then, but she isn't sure where to start. I was never that much interested in history. Seemed sort of dry and boring to me. It might be kind of fun to research the family."

"If you want, I can send you some names and addresses of genealogy places that help you trace your family," Jenny said. "I will warn you, though, it can become addictive."

"Mom would appreciate that," Rand said. "Give her something to do in the evenings, when she gets tired of quilting."

The town of Red Bluffs spread out before them as the topped the last ridge and dropped into a wide valley at the base of the mountains.

"Whew," Jenny said. "I am literally dying for a cup of coffee. Can I buy you one for your troubles. Or breakfast?" Her stomach felt empty. A sweet roll would be heavenly.

"I never turn down coffee," Rand said. "There's a Perkins on this end of town."

"Great," Jenny said. "Then I'll call Triple A about getting my car towed in."

The Perkins was crowded, but the hostess found them a table. The breakfast smells tickled Jenny's nose, and her stomach again reminded her that breakfast was certainly in order.

When the coffee came, Jenny thought nothing had ever tasted so good.

She drained one cup, and smiled at Rand when he raised an eyebrow. "I usually drink coffee first thing, I feel deprived."

Rand grinned when the croissant came, and Jenny smiled back, but didn't let his amusement stop her from eating. "I didn't have much to eat in my car last night, so I'm hungry." She explained.

"I can tell," Rand said, drinking on his second cup of coffee.

After she finished with the flaky croissant, Jenny felt better. The coffee helped too. After she paid the bill, she held out her hand, and Rand took it in a firm handshake. It was purely a thank-you gesture, and there was no reason for the thrill that danced through her at the touch of his work-roughened hand.

His brown eyes studied her for a moment, but there was no way of knowing if he felt the same at her touch.

"Thanks for the coffee," Rand said. "Are you sure you'll be okay?"

"Yes, thanks again. I just have to call the AAA towing service and get the car back to town, and I saw Firestone just down the street."

Rand pulled a leather wallet with a longhorn head tooled on it out of his hip pocket, and handed her a business card.

"That's my home phone and cell number, if you have any trouble call me. The address is there too, if you get around to mailing mom that genealogy stuff. Dad knows a lot of the history around here, and Henry does too. Maybe you could talk to them as well."

"Sounds like a good idea. I planned to interview some of the residents here, and they would be a good start."

Jenny reached into her purse, took a business card out of her billfold and handed it to Rand.

"Here's my card too, if your dad or Henry have anything that might help, I would appreciate them letting me know."

"Well, if you'll be okay, I'll take off," Rand said

"Again, thanks for all your help," Jenny said, and watched him walk out of the restaurant, admiring his broad shoulders and lean hips encased in tight fitting Levi jeans. Even with his modern clothing, Jenny knew that had he been dressed in a homespun shirt and trousers, he would be a twin to the man in her dream.

She looked at the card he had given her. "Logan Longhorns and Roping Stock, The <u>WL</u> brand means generations of know how behind each cow," She noticed that his father's name was Waylyn. A rather unusual name, Jenny thought. Then she dropped the card in her billfold, found a seat next to the restaurant's landscaping and dialed the 800 number on her AAA card to find a tow truck.

Then she called the local Firestone Store, so she could use her Firestone card, and luckily the man said he could work on her Explorer later in the day.

The tow truck driver had been agreeable to picking her up at the Perkins, and she found him to be a chatty companion on the ride out to retrieve her vehicle.

At the Firestone store, the counterman agreed to give her a ride to the library and pick her up when the vehicle was fixed. She had to research anyway, so she didn't feel as if the breakdown was a complete waste of time.

The Wyoming room was full of books concerned with Wyoming history, Jenny found some background material on Red Bluffs and Crystal Creek. Knowing she could get the books through the inner library loan system, she jotted down the titles and the author, but took notes just in case. She talked to the librarian, and the lady told her they had extensive microfilm of the old newspapers, which Jenny knew would be her best resource.

She did find one interesting item in the old papers. Barney Morgan had homesteaded near Wild Rose, so it was a good bet that the 'old Morgan place' was Barney's homestead.

She asked the reference librarian if there were any books showing homestead plats, and was directed to a book of Crystal Creek history, where she found a section map and Barney Morgan's homestead listed on it. Jenny copied down the range, township and section the homestead was located in. She suspected that Henry Frost would know the sections. Another look at the map showed that the Logan homestead and the Frost homestead joined the Morgan homestead so it was a good bet that it was right one.

Two hours flew by, and Jenny asked the research assistant for a recommendation on a place to eat lunch. They recommended Bradfords, a sports bar and restaurant just two blocks away.

It was two o'clock when the Firestone mechanic called to say her SUV was ready, and they would meet pick her up in front of the library.

She was even surprised and pleased to find that the bill was less than she expected, and she thanked the counter man as she paid with her Firestone card. She was glad to have the Explorer up and running; they had replaced the fuel pump, and she filled the tank with gas at the Holiday gas station, decided she might as well try to contact Henry and see the homestead.

A gruff voice answered when she dialed the number. She told him about her dilemma.

"Sure, come on out. Elsie will be

glad to show you around. Not much left though. Just ruins." Henry said.

Jenny assured the shaky, querulous voice that she was interested in the ruins, and the man gave her directions to his place.

It was getting late by the time Jenny pulled in the driveway of the weathered ranch house, needing a coat of paint and a some new poles on the fence around the yard, but the large cottonwood trees were heavy with green leaves, and the garden plot, fenced off from the driveway area, had green curls of lettuce, and spears of corn.

A woman about Jenny's age was working on staking some tomato plants, that looked like they would like to fall over without such help. The woman waved a friendly hand when she saw

Jenny's car, and came over to the wooden gate that allowed entrance to the garden plot.

"You must be the gal from Billings. My name's Elsie. Gramps said you were looking for an old homestead. Rand called earlier as well. Gramps is doctoring a heifer. She didn't shed the afterbirth right. But I can take you out there. No problem."

Jenny took the offered hand. "Jenny Morgan . Yes, I need some photos of the old Morgan place."

"Road's pretty rough. We'll take the Dodge. Your SUV looks too pretty to get all muddied up." She grinned.

Jenny took her camera and notepad from the passenger seat of the Explorer, decided against locking it, she had her billfold, car keys, her camera in the camera bag, and there was nothing else worth stealing anyway. Besides, ranch people were usually as honest as they came.

She followed Elsie to the ancient, battered four-door Dodge and waited while the other girl cleaned jackets, halters and bridles off the seat; boots and feed sacks off the floor, tossing all into the back seat, which was piled high with saddles and saddle blankets.

"Ranch truck," Elsie explained. "Anything else on the floor, step on. Won't hurt it."

Jenny wasn't worried about hurting the stuff, which appeared to a grease gun and an oily rag, but it looked dusty and greasy and she was worried about what grease might do to her white tennis shoes. Oh well, they were cheap, Wal-Mart specials. She could always buy new ones. Still, she kept her feet as far from the grease gun as possible.

"I appreciate this. I talked to Rand Logan this morning, he kind of rescued me when my car wouldn't start. I was taking pictures of Wild Rose yesterday, and when I mentioned Barney Morgan he told me about this homestead. So I wanted photos of that too."

"Rand told me about your project. Sounds interesting." the girl shifted gears smoothly and turned unto a rough back road that looked like two parallel trails.

"Have you lived here long? Rand said his family has lived here for over 100 years."

"My mom was raised here. She moved away, got married, then we moved back when I was in high school.

Our ranch isn't as old as Rand's, but Gramps homesteaded here in the 20's so that's quite awhile.   Rand and I graduated together. He's a great guy."

They bumped along the rutted back road, Elsie said the Dodge had no air conditioning, so the smell of dust and sage drifted through the open pickup windows. Ahead was a wire gate, and when Elsie stopped Jenny stepped out to open it so they could drive through.

"Leave it open," Elsie said. "No cows around."

A line of trees indicated a small stream down a long, grassy slope. Near the creek Jenny could see the dilapidated shell of a log cabin, the windows looking like empty eye-sockets.

"There it is, what's left of it," Elsie

waved a hand towards the cabin and turned off the two-track and drove across the grass flat, pulling up beside the ruin.

Elsie stopped the pickup and they both got out. "Take all the photos you want. But watch for rattlers. Grandpa killed a big one under the house earlier this summer."

Snakes again. Jenny wished she had worn hiking boots or better yet, knee-high ones. She hated snakes, and rattlesnakes in particular. Elsie let the way to the cabin, and pushed open the door. It creaked as it opened, scraping along the plank floor.

Jenny took some photos, outside, nervously starting whenever a grasshopper trilled in the weeds, sounding like a rattlesnake. Then she followed Elsie inside.

The cabin had wood floors, which meant that the owner was a little more prosperous than many homesteaders, who only had dirt floors. Now, the floors creaked and sagged underfoot.

Standing in lonely splendor in what was once the kitchen was an old cast- iron cook stove, probably left because it was too heavy to take along when Barney moved into town. There was no other furniture, not even an old bedstead.

It was a sad place really. Jenny took several photos, feeling a kinship with the place. Her great-great-grandfather had lived here. He was getting more and more real to her the more she researched his life.

Near the door was a stand of red poppies, and a wild rose bush in full bloom near the door. Jenny took a photo of them, with the house as a background.

She wondered who had planted them, and why they still lived.

"Got enough?" Elsie asked as Jenny put her camera back in the bag and zipped it up.

"I think so. It was nice of you to take the time to drive me out here. Can I pay you, for gas or anything?"

"Nah, I enjoyed it. Its not often something happens around here and this was better than mopping floors or weeding. Anywhere else you want to go?" she asked hopefully.

Jenny laughed. "No, this was all I needed here. I sure appreciate you taking me out here, but I have to get back. I plan to be back home tonight, and it's getting late." The sun was low in the sky, but it stayed light until after 8, and Jenny didn't mind driving after dark anyway.

Elsie turned the pickup around and they headed back to her ranch.

At the Frost ranch, Jenny thanked Elsie again and drove back down the gravel road towards Red Bluffs and home.

After a stop in Red Bluffs for a cold drink, she turned onto I-90 and headed north. She was rather sorry to see Red Bluffs dip out of sight in her rear-view mirror, and she didn't want to think about her experience in the ghost town. She didn't want to think about Wolf's chocolate-brown eyes, or Rand's, nearly the same color. The necklace was cool against her skin, and she remembered Wolf saying he would always be back.

She turned on the radio, tuning in to a country music station, knowing it would soon fade out as she drove out of the range of the radio signal. She wondered why leaving Wyoming gave her an empty feeling, as if she were leaving the place that she belonged.

Chapter 6
Present

Back in Billings, in her small house, Jenny opened her laptop, and set about entering the data from her note pad into the computer, and downloading the photos from her SD card. They turned out well, but she wished she had been able to take photos of the ghost town as it had looked in her dream. But, maybe the dream had no basic on reality.

She pulled up what she had accumulated so far on Barney Morgan. Barney Morgan, born, 1860, in Ashe County, North Carolina, where he studied law and came to Wyoming in 1883 as a young man. He took up a homestead near Wild Rose and was elected as a territorial sheriff the next year.

There were a lot of stories about his sheriff days, and Jenny enjoyed reading of his adventures, planning to include them in the book. Later, he became a judge, and moved to Red Bluffs, and years after that was elected as a senator of the newly organized state.

He had married late in life, he was 38 when he met and married a Kathy Sanders in Red Bluffs, on July 25, 1886. Witnesses, Mr. Pratt and a Mrs. Ellis. Barney's parents were named, but Kathy Sanders had no parents mentioned.

Jenny had never met her great grandparents, they had died before she was born. Even her grandmother, who she remembered as a tiny, white-haired lady, and died when Jenny was young.

Maybe Kathy was an orphan. Maybe she had been part of one of the Orphan's Trains, that brought children west from places like New York. Jenny made a note on her research to look into Kathy Sanders, surely there was something about her, other than her marriage license.

In addition to the facts Jenny had learned in Cheyenne and in Crystal Creek, she included her impressions of the town of Wild Rose, and the countryside surrounding the homestead ruins themselves.

The strange dream kept intruding on her thoughts as she typed. Finally, in aggravation, Jenny closed out her research notes and typed in everything she could remember about her dream.

It read almost like a chapter in a

historical novel. The details were rich and believable, and Wolf's character dominated the scene.

Although he was not Jenny's idea of a romantic hero, thinking about his tall, spare body made a thrill run through her again as she relived the dream. She hadn't met many men like him, strong yet capable of tenderness to those they loved. Men who were men, and in charge of every situation. She wasn't even sure where such thoughts came from, as she didn't remember that from the dream, it was just the aura that Wolf projected.

Rand Logan's face formed in the back of her mind. Well, maybe there was one. Rand, she felt, would definitely be in charge in any situation.

The phone rang, and Jenny jumped.

She checked the caller id and then picked up the phone. "Hi Mom, how are you?"

"Oh, you are home. Did you have a

good trip?"

"Yes, I did. Except for the breakdown," Jenny said.

"Glad it was successful. I wondered if you wanted to come to supper tonight, there's someone I'd like you to meet. Her name is Louise Benson, she spoke last week at my Woman's Club meeting. I invited her over for supper. She reads palms and auras. She's very interesting."

"Sound's like fun," Jenny said. "Want me to come around 6?" Six was the usual time for her family to eat supper.

"Around there. We might eat about 7 or so. Could you swing by the super market and pick me up some fresh ginger? I have powdered but fresh is better."

"No problem," Jenny said. "See you then."

She hung up the phone, smiling. Her mother was interested in everything, from historical architecture to zen. She often reminded Jenny of a honeybee, flitting from one flower to another. This week it was palm and aura reading, last month it was water witching and growing herbs. One thing about it, her mother was never dull.

Louise Benson was easy to like, Jenny thought as she talked to her over the delicious dinner her mother prepared. Short and rather plump, dressed in gray slacks and a tailored shirt, Louise didn't look like a fortune teller, more like a professional church woman.

After supper, Marlene, Jenny's mother, suggested that Jenny show Louis the garden, as Louis was an expert on herbs and medicinal plants. "By the time you get back, dessert will be ready," Marlene said.

After they left the house, Louise said. "You have something to ask me."

Jenny, surprised, recounted her dream, wondering if Louise would tell her it was just a dream, give her some Jungian interpretation, and talk of dream symbols. Instead, she was silent for a moment.

"Your aura," she said, and her eyes had a faraway look. "Your aura is overshadowed. I can see you, and another spirit overshadowing your own. It is difficult, they are shimmering, moving, in and out. First you, then another you. A you of, perhaps, another time, another place. Another Jenny."

As if coming out of a trance, Louise shook herself.

"What do you mean, another Jenny?" Jenny asked, intrigued.

"We have all lived before," Louise said. "For the most part, before we are born again to this plane, the memories are wiped out completely, so the past does not intrude on the present. In your case, the lives seem to be closer together. Perhaps a past life was left unfinished, and now it needs completion. Perhaps you will finish the cycle that has begun. However, the answer may take awhile to find. Have you ever heard about holograms? About the entire universe being a hologram?"

The concept was new to Jenny. She admitted she had never heard of it.

"Study it. It might help you understand. Now, let us look at your mother's herbs. I was interested in seeing her many flavors of mint."

Jenny lead Louise to the herb garden, her mother's pride. She loved the smell of the mints on the summer breeze, and found she recognized many of them from her mother's lectures and her own study.

"Ginger mint, the variegated one, is good in rhubarb pie and rhubarb crisp," Jenny said. "And I really like the chocolate mint in a lot of desserts." She bent over the herbs, and the necklace fell forward, and Louise saw it for the first time.

"I love your necklace," Louise said. "Turquoise is a very powerful mineral. Protects, heals, and increases your spiritual vibrations. May I touch it?"

Jenny took off the necklace and dropped it into Louise's hand. The older lady ran her hands across the rough stones.

"You did not buy this. It was given to you by a lover, no?"

"Well, not really." Jenny said, and explained how she had found the necklace after she had the dream.

"This necklace belonged to two women before you. One was very evil. The other, she is you, yet she is not you. This necklace has seen much sorrow, but now it has come home."

Louise handed it back to her and they walked a short distance and then Louise said. "I see roses. Wild roses.

Does this make sense?"

Jenny stopped, surprised. "The name of the ghost town was Wild Rose."

"You have to go back there. There, you will find the answers. You will also find....Oh, hello Marlene. I'm sorry we are taking so long. I love the mints. Jenny let me taste the chocolate mint, can I get a cutting?"

"Of course," Marlene said. "Dessert is ready, shall we go inside."

They walked back to the house together, and Jenny thought about what Louise had said. She, too, felt the call of the old town, and the strangeness of the dream. Yes, she had to go back.

Her mind made up, she followed Louise and Marlene back into the house.

Chapter 7
Present

It was late when she got back to her apartment. The talk with Louise had been interesting, if rather disconcerting.   She took off the necklace and laid it gently in her jewelry box. She knew had to go back to Wild Rose. She had to find the answers.

The next day she called the paper in Red Bluffs, Wyoming and put in an ad about finding the necklace, actually hoping that no one would claim it. She was getting rather attached to it.

When she picked up her mail later in the day there was a letter from the Wyoming Historical Society, that they had received another grant, and that they could pay her more than they had originally proposed for her book. That was great news. It would give her more than enough money to live in Crystal Creek and do her research for three months.

"Fate," her mother would have said.

"Sheer coincidence," would have been her father's opinion. If nothing else, he was a realist. Maybe they were both right.

A week later, Jenny had everything ready to move to Wyoming. Through a realtor, she found a small house with rent she could afford.

It had taken her a little over a week, but finally Jenny had everything loaded in the Explorer, with her laptop computer riding in the place of honor on the front seat, and she was ready to go.

It seemed as if a little voice inside her head was saying, "Hurry, hurry,"

The drive from Billings was pleasant, the day was warm and windy, blowing the tall grass along the roadside like white-green ocean waves. White puffy clouds rode high above, contrasting pleasantly with the blue sky.

When she got to Red Bluffs the first order of business was to find the realtor, as Crystal Creek was too small to have such amenities, settle up on the rental, and get directions to it.

The realtor, Nita Browne, was happy to get out of the office for the day, said she would take her car and meet Jenny at the Crystal Creek post office.

Jenny approved of the house. It was an older house, sat some distance from the road, with a back yard full of huge cottonwood trees. Jenny especially liked the many-paned entry door, that let in the sunlight.

It was partially furnished, and Jenny found that 'partially furnished' meant an older propane stove, a table, two chairs, an iron-framed bed, with, the realtor told her, a new mattress, and a fairly new sofa. It smelled of pine sol, and everything looked clean. It would do for the summer.

"It looks great," Jenny told Nita. "We discussed $500 a month, right?" she dug in her shoulder bag and withdrew her black and white snow leopard print check book.

"First and last months in advance," Nita said.

Jenny laughed. "I'll only be here for three months. How about the entire amount."

Nita shrugged. "Works for me."

After Jenny assured Nita that she

didn't need help getting settled in, Nita left.

After sighing a little thinking about the work of settling in, she began to unload the Explorer. Laptop, clothes, bedding; television; pots and pans. The house only had one bedroom, so she set up her computer on the kitchen table.

Thinking about having a glass of iced tea, she dug out her ice cube trays and tea bags and glass pitcher. She took a drink of the tap water, it cool and good with no hint of chlorine. Well water, not city water.

She filled the ice cube trays and put them in old-fashioned freezer above the fridge, and ran a pitcher full of water for sun-tea.

It didn't take long to set up housekeeping. At least Billings wasn't that far away, and Jenny could go back on weekends and pick up forgotten supplies. Like her crock-pot. And cookbooks.

As evening drew near, Jenny finished her unpacking and settling in. For some reason, she felt sick. Like a touch of a flu, or food poisoning. She had been fine earlier. Maybe it was just the rush of packing and unpacking.

The ice cubes weren't frozen yet, so she ran another glass of water from the tap, and put the sun tea, now brewed to a dark caramel brown, in the fridge. Then she lay down on the sofa, and wished she had called the satellite company to hook in the Dish Network receiver on the house to get some television channels.

She had some DVD's, and a portable player, but none of the movies interested her. She settled on a romance book instead.

Her stomach still roiled, and it felt like fear. But of what? The conversation with Rand came back to her. She wondered if this was one of the haunted houses, and suddenly wished she hadn't been so quick to pay up the rent. She wondered what Nita would have said if she had insisted in sleeping in the house first. That probably would not have worked.

The shadows were getting longer, and Jenny turned on some lights to keep the dark at bay. The feeling of unease grew stronger as the day drew to a close.

A voice seemed to be whispering in her brain, "Wild Rose, Wild Rose." Suddenly, the house seemed filled with the slightly musky rose scent.

"Wild Rose." The turquoise necklace, which Jenny had forgotten that she was wearing, suddenly seemed cold. Ice cold. Jenny unhooked it and jerked it off. The blue stones seemed to glow faintly. There seemed to be a pulling at her mind, like the pull on her body when she had been drawn into a tiny whirlpool one time while swimming in a creek.

The pull became stronger and

stronger, and she knew she had to get to Wild Rose.

Once she settled herself in the car and headed towards the ghost town, the feeling stopped. Her stomach settled down and the insistent call was more like a distance echo in her head. Jenny felt as if she had been in the grip of something stronger than any human endurance.

Jenny wondered what would happen if she turned around and headed back home, but she didn't feel courageous enough to fight against the pull. Whatever might await her in the ghost town might not be as bad as the feeling of being controlled by something she didn't understand.

Chapter 8
1885

A knock sounded on the door. Jen started, turning from the coal stove and gathering up her skirt. She opened the door.

The man on the porch was of medium height and strongly built. He had a fringe of dark hair under a narrow brimmed hat. The evening shadows made his face difficult to see.

"Hello. Miss Jen?"

She nodded.

"I need to find Wolf Logan. He asked me to meet him here tonight." Seeing her startled glance, he added. "We are old friends. May I come in?"

Jen looked at him for a moment, suddenly decided to trust him. He didn't look like an outlaw, he looked and spoke like an English gentleman. He didn't have a side arm, and she had seen no sign of any other weapon either.

"Of course." She stepped back out of the way. "Wolf isn't here, but if he told you to meet him, I guess he will be here shortly. Could I offer you a cup of coffee?"

"Thank you, yes. That would be excellent."

They drank the coffee in silence, Jen was afraid to say too much about Wolf, not knowing what the man wanted. He didn't talk, didn't ask any questions, but sipped his coffee and seemed content with the silence. Jen wondered if he were listening for Wolf's approach, just as she was. The silence was all-encompassing, and Jen was so glad to hear hoof-beats that she almost ran to the door, glad to see it was Wolf on his long legged black horse. The man was relaxed at the table, acting as comfortable as if he were in his own house.

Wolf swung out of the saddle, glanced at the other man's horse tied to the porch railing, then strode inside.

"Judge," Wolf acknowledged his presence.

"Wolf." The man nodded.

"Coffee." Wolf said, with barely a glance at Jen, but she already had a stoneware mug ready with the strong, hot brew. She handed it to him without a word, but his eyes acknowledged her and a half smile flitted across his face. Then he turned his attention back to the stranger.

"You needed to see me?" Wolf

asked.

"Yes, indeed, I have a very special favor to ask of you. You remember Lord Greylion, who came to this country about, oh, three years ago?"

"He has a large ranch down south. He's related to some English royalty."

The other man nodded. "He is from a fine old family in England. He plans to send a shipment to be presented to the territorial governor. It is a very rare and expensive silver and jewel inlaid candelabra for the governor's mansion. It is guarded, but additional guards may be necessary, especially after it is transferred to the Overland Stage line. And most especially if what we believe about our friend is true."

Wolf stroked his chin. He hadn't shaved for several days, and had a heavy shadow of dark whiskers.

"Anything new?" Wolf asked.

The   man   shook   his   head.

"Nothing. A lot of suspicions, no facts."

"I'm sure he knows about the shipment."

"Undoubtedly. Telegrams have been sent to every official in our territory, warning them to make sure nothing happens to it."

"As usual." Wolf agreed. "That might be good. He has to get word to his partners. If I follow one of them, we can get the proof we need to keep this robbery from happening."

"Very good. Don't take chances, but I'm counting on you. So far, you've gotten closer to him than anyone else has, and I agree with your conclusions. But, a jury would need proof, and that is what we do not have."

To Jenny, the talk meant very little, except that Wolf would be risking his life, again, against someone who was bound to rob the stage.

"We need Arizona," Wolf was

saying. "He's the link. I believe that our friend is using him and his band to help with the robberies. I'm sure we can convince him to talk, if we can catch him."

"I know you have personal reasons for wanting Arizona. But, you could be right about his involvement in the robberies. Get the proof, however you have to go about it."

"If I bring Arizona in, will there be another 'escape?'" Wolf asked sarcastically.

"I have sent word to Cheyenne for the United States Marshall. He will be here within the week, with plans to stay for a least a month. There will be no escape this time."

"Where can I contact you if I get the information?"

"I will be in Rocky Point. You can send a telegraph from Red Bluffs, but not from here. If what we believe is true, they know everything that goes in and out of Wild Rose."

Wolf nodded, rubbing his chin again. "I'll rest here tonight, and be on the trail early in the morning."

The shorter man rose and shook hands with Wolf, tipped his hat to Jen, and disappeared into the soft summer night.

"You have to leave tomorrow." Jen said. It was a statement, not a question.

"Yes. I'm getting closer. The information we discussed tonight may help confirm what I suspected. I can't tell you anything more. If our hunch proves correct, all hell will break loose here in Wild Rose soon.

"You mean with Jesse Arizona?"

"Him and others." Wolf paused, staring out the small window over the wash pans, draining upside down on the shelf. "One man. One man here in Wild Rose that I can't touch, that I can't bring in across the saddle. We are sure he is behind every crooked thing that happens in this part of the territory. How else could Arizona and his band know exactly which stage carried the gold, which stages the payroll shipments are on?" He paused, looking at Jen. She didn't say anything, and he went on.

"Someone is giving them that information. Arizona never holds up the mail stages unless he knows there are valuables on board. Stealing this shipment would be a great achievement for him. We cannot allow him to steal it. The robbery, if it happened, would have negative ramifications for the entire territory. It might even affect the plans others are setting in motion for statehood."

He was talking to himself, rather than to her, Jen knew. She kept silent, watching him.

"That man who was here, he is an

old friend, we have worked together before. Right now, he is the only man I can trust. If something happens to me, and he comes to you, do whatever he says, go wherever he tells you to go." He reached out to her, cupping her chin in his work-roughed hands. "Now, let's not waste the rest of the night."

He put his arms around her and pulled her close. Bending down, he gently kissed her lips, and Jenny returned the kiss, giving herself to the feeling he aroused in her. A warmth rushed through her that had nothing to do with the warm night or even the warmth of his lean body against hers.

"Let's go to bed," she whispered. "I want you."

"And I need to hold my woman before I have to go out again," Wolf said. Still holding her in one arm, he reached over and turned the down the wick of the lamp, watching the flame wink out. The moonlight left silver streaks on the wood floor.

In the bedroom at the back of the house Jen slipped out of her dress and began to undo the lacing of her camisole. Wolf stripped off his travel worn clothes, and stretched out full length on the bed, watching as she undid the lacing and slowly slid the lacy undergarment off her shoulders, and then took the pins out of her hair, shaking out the long, golden-brown tresses.

She loved the look of Wolf's naked body, the moonlight playing across the hard planes of his chest, and his long, muscular legs. She lay down beside him, throwing one arm across him, and moving her lips up to his.

He kissed her, than put his lips to the soft skin on her neck, worrying the skin. The moonlight bathed them both in soft, white light, and somewhere an owl called.

Chapter 9
Present

The owls were asleep. Sunlight tickled Jenny Morgan's eyes and she opened them briefly, then closed them against the bright glare. She could still feel Wolf's arms around her, still feel his hands roving across her body. She was in love. In love with a fantasy, a dream, a wisp of nothingness.

But he had been so solid, so real in her dream. She could still taste his kisses, whiskey mingled with coffee. Lightning forked through her chest as she remembered every detail of their lovemaking.

She examined her face in her rear view mirror, looking for any sign of what had happened. There was a small red mark on her throat, and she remembered Wolf's lips on her neck. She sank back into the car seat. Wolf's brand. A remembrance of her lover and their love-making. He came to her as a dream but was real enough to leave the mark of his presence.

Leaning back and closing her eyes, Jenny opened her mind to recall the dream.

The other man, the one who had given Wolf the information about the upcoming stage robbery had looked vaguely familiar, why, Jenny didn't know.

She also wondered who they had been referring to, the man who gave Jesse

Arizona the information on the stages that carried the gold.

By the way they talked, the other man sounded like a law officer, and it surprised Jenny to find that Wolf was working within the law, instead of outside it's boundaries. Bounty hunters, she thought, worked alone, and were often considered only a little less lawless than the men they pursued. Strange.

However, they did go after the lawless element, so they could be, sort of, considered some of the good guys in the old west, but often the line between bad and good was pretty blurry.

The sound a vehicle coming her way roused Jenny from her thoughts. "Oh, God," she thought as she recognized the maroon Chevrolet pickup, and the driver. She wanted to sink down into her car seat. What would he think, finding her here again at such an early hour? At least she wasn't broke down, or at least she hoped she wasn't.

The pickup stopped behind her car and Rand Logan got out. Again, she was struck by the resemblance between him and Wolf. Had the man called him Wolf Logan in her dream? She was sure that was the name.

But, maybe, however, her mind had supplied a last name. Wolf was probably only a product of her dreaming mind, and it had merely set Rand in the Old West, because he was the most attractive man she had seen in years.

Rand's grin was wide as he looked at her.

"Well, hello Jenny from Billings. Are you broke down again, in the exact same spot? We have to quit meeting like this, you know. People might start to talk."

Jenny looked up and down the deserted road. "What people?"

"Oh, there are some in the area.

However, you being from the heavily populated state of Montana, it must look very desolate to you."

"Heavily populated my eye. Montana ranks close to Wyoming in being the least populated state, and is almost even in population density." Jenny answered.

"Right you are. But Billings is a major population center for this area, so this road must seem very deserted."

"It seems to be. Where are you going, again, so early in the a of m?" Jenny asked.

"To the auto supply store in Red Bluffs. A belt on the one of our trucks snapped and I was elected to drive to town for a new one. If you like, and if you vehicle will start, I'll buy you a cup of coffee at the Cenex cafe. How's that for class?"

Jenny laughed. "Very classy. Red Bluff's answer to the Ritz Carlton I presume."

"Not quite. For that we have The Sharpshooter Restaurant, or the Golden Steer. Both have excellent food."

"I see. I'll try them out someday, but as for now, I'll meet you at Cenex for that coffee."

She turned the key in the ignition and the SUV started without a hitch. She fell in behind Rand's pickup and followed him the remaining 20 miles to Red Bluffs.

The Cenex cafe, attached to a truck stop, was not exactly the Ritz Carlton, but the coffee was hot and strong.

Rand took a drink of coffee, then looked at Jenny. She knew what was coming.

"Now," Rand said. "The first time you broke down at Wild Rose. This time, what is your reasoning. You were either up very early and drove out to watch the sun rise over the ruins, or you spent the night there in your car. Why?"

Even during the 20 minute drive to Red Bluffs, Jenny hadn't thought up a convincing lie. She tried the side-track method.

"Is Wolf Logan related to you?" She asked bluntly.

If Rand felt surprise he kept it hidden. "He was my great-great-grandfather. His homestead ruins are out on the ranch."

Jenny knew she would like to see Wolf's homestead sometime, but she didn't yet know Rand well enough to ask for that favor. She was glad he invited her for coffee today, maybe she could get to know him. She told herself he was essential to her research, not that he was a good looking and a cowboy.

"What does my great-great-grandfather have to do with you spending the night in the ghost town?" Rand asked when Jenny didn't answer his first question.

The side-track method hadn't worked. Jenny felt put on the spot, but decided to come clean. If he thought she was crazy, so be it, but she knew it was always better to tell the truth than to have to remember a lie. Perhaps the truth was less crazy than any lie she could invent anyway.

"Both times I was in the ghost town, I had dreams about the town being just as it was in 1885. In the first dream I saw a calendar behind the bar with that date. In the dreams I'm a woman named Jen, and her lover is a bounty hunter named Wolf Logan, who is chasing an outlaw named Jesse Arizona."

Rand shook his head. Jenny could see the surprise in his face. "You've got to be kidding. There was an outlaw named Jesse Arizona, he was famous, or infamous, around here. I don't know if Wolf was chasing him or not, and I don't know if Wolf was a bounty hunter. No one has ever said much about Wolf, I got the impression that he was the black sheep of our family."

Jenny laughed. " But not a sheep in Wolf's clothing I take it."

Rand grinned. "I guess you could say that. I just got the impression that he was a wild character. Our family never has cared much about tracing our family tree. I guess we're afraid we'll find some bad apples hanging on it."

Jenny was reassured by Rand's humor, but felt a slight chill when she realized that both Wolf and Jesse had actually lived. How could she have known? Dreams were suppose to be symbols and facets of one's subconscious mind, but how could her mind have dredged up two, and for all she knew, maybe more, ghosts of the past that she had no prior knowledge of?

"Are you sure Wolf Logan and Jesse

Arizona didn't come up in your research? The only way you knew the names was through the dreams?   That's kind of weird."

Weird was one word for it, Jenny thought. Eerie was another one.

"I'm positive," Jenny said. "I've never researched Wolf or Jesse Arizona, why would I?   I've been researching Barney Morgan.   Those names never came up in my research at all. "

"You said you don't know much about Wolf, but he must have had at least one son somewhere," she felt a smile tug at her lips.   "Because it is a proven fact if your grandparents didn't have kids, you won't either. Sort of a genetic link there."

Rand grinned at the rather lame joke. "My great-grandfather, Phelan, was raised by two very straight-laced aunts. When he got older he became a circuit-riding preacher, hell-fire and brimstone and lots of Satan. I guess he converted a lot of people in his day, scared 'em into converting, I think. Pa said he was a big man, with a long white beard, but Santa Claus he wasn't! He used to scare Pa to death as a kid with his visions of hell-fire. I guess he could really have made you believe in any savior he picked out. I guess that's why my family has always been church goers. His son, JR, wasn't as radical, but he went to church every Sunday."

He laughed, a little abashed, Jenny thought. But, he hadn't seemed ashamed to admit it.

"Phelen must have been married to have a son," Jenny said, curious about the rest of the story.

Rand shrugged. "I guess the story was he met my grandma at a revival meeting, and fell in love with her. He was an old geezer I guess, and she was only 25, but it must have been love. She agreed to marry him if he gave up circuit riding and settled down. The aunts had paid the taxes on Wolf's homestead when Phelean was young. When he quit riding he took it over, became a rancher, and raised four kids. His son, JR, was my grandfather. Pa was his only son so he inherited the ranch."

He took a drink of his coffee, and grinned. "Funny what a woman can do to a man, isn't it?"

Jenny laughed. "Yeah, it is, but usually they quit drinking and carousing, not preaching."

"He didn't quit preaching, just riding. He started the first Methodist church in Crystal Creek, preached there off and on until he died."

It was a revelation. Wolf Logan, a bounty hunter, but having a son that grew up to be a hell-fire Billy Sunday preacher sounded completely at odds with each other. But, Rand had said Phelan was raised by his aunts.

Phelan was an unusual name as well, but in the 1800's odd names were the rule, not the exception.

"Phelan was Wolf's son, then? So Wolf had a wife?"

Rand shrugged. "I guess he would have had to, to have a son. But I really don't know much about him. I never knew great-grandpa, he died before I was born. My granddad, Phelan Jr., everyone called him J.R., took over the ranch, and Pa carried on after him."

He drained his coffee cup and shook his head when the waitress offered him a refill. "I gotta go. Dad will have a cow if I'm too late with the belt. Come on out anytime, I know Mom would like to talk to you about tracing our roots. I'm kind of curious myself about Wolf, now that you brought the subject up."

"Thanks for the coffee, Rand. I appreciate it and I appreciate you listening to me about the dreams. By the way, Elsie took me to his homestead. It was Barney's I checked it on the homestead plat map. Thanks."

"Good. I'm glad it was the right one? See you later."

"I hope you don't get in trouble for being late with the belt."

"No worries. It was good to see you again," Rand said, and his smile made Jenny feel warm inside, as if they had shared an intimate moment. The dream came back to her, and Wolf's face. His smile had lit his brown eyes exactly as Rand's smile did.

Chapter 10
Present

After Rand left the cafe, Jenny had two choices. Either go back to Crystal Creek or do some more research at the Red Bluff's library, since she was in town anyway.

She wanted to look at the microfiche of old newspapers, and research in some of the rarer books in the Wyoming's History Room, books which could not be checked out.

The newspapers were disappointing, but she did find one news story that she photocopied, "Barney Morgan, District Court Judge, was honored by the governor today for being a leading figure in cleaning up the corruption that had been an accepted part of Red Bluffs and Wild Rose for several years. 'Although Mr. Morgan hired many people of less than reputable reputations, with their help he accomplished what he hoped to do, and in doing so brought several people to justice. Wyoming is honored to have him as a part of our justice system,' the governor said in the ceremony, which was held at the State Capital."

She wished the article would have mentioned more names, but maybe Barney had known that naming the others would endanger their lives. Still, for the modern researcher, it left many gaps in knowledge.

Her eyes began to tire, so she shut off the machine and found several books about the area, she photocopied the information she thought might be helpful. One book that was a part of the general collection titled *Old Settler Trails* mentioned Barney Morgan and Wild Rose several times.

She had found nothing about Wolf Logan, and had Rand not said Wolf was his great-great-grandfather, she would have doubted the reality of him.

Having found her research books, she decided she couldn't research all the time. With the help of the computer, she found the paranormal section and picked out several books on dreams, past lives and reincarnation.

The librarian, a dark haired girl about Jenny's age, smiled as she looked at the eclectic selection.

Jenny grinned back. "These are research," she pointed to the historic books.   "These are my leisure time reading." she added, "I'm working on a book about my great-great-grandfather for the Wyoming Historical Society. He lived in this area, he was a sheriff and a judge, and later went on to be a state senator."

"Sounds interesting. Let us know when it is published. My name is Laura, I usually work the research desk. I'll be happy to help you any way I can."

"I'm Jenny Morgan." she held out her hand and Laura returned her handshake. "I'm sure I'll be here a lot. Thanks. I appreciate that. Nice to meet you," Jenny said, gathering up the books.

"You too," Laura said.   Jenny smiled at her and walked out.

When Jenny got back to her rented house, there was a familiar looking battered pickup in the driveway, and Jenny recognized the girl that jumped out as she drove up and got out of the car.

Elsie, that was her name. The girl that took her to Barney's homestead.

"Hey, Jenny. Hi. Thought I'd drop by and see how things are going. Flora, she knows everything that goes on in town, told me that you had rented the old Duncan place and you were doing some research. You busy?"

"No," Jenny said, reaching inside the car again to get the books. "I just got back from Red Bluffs library, doing some research."

"We have a small branch library here," Elsie said. "Do you need help?"

"Thanks. I've got it. I've just got these books. Want to come in? I've got some tea brewed if you would like a glass."

"Sounds   good,"   Elsie   said, following Jenny inside.

"This is kind of a cute house. I'd never been inside."

"It's small but good enough for

me," Jenny said, as she poured two glasses of tea.

"What are your plans for the day," Elsie asked after she took a drink of tea.

"I was going to work some, I wanted to enter my research into my computer," Jenny said, sitting down across the table from Elsie.

"Darn.   I was thinking, well, hoping, I mean, most of my school friends are married or gone, and I was kind of hoping you would be bored out of your skull here, and would want to ride along with me to Rand Logan's ranch. Some of his cows got into our pasture, and I have to haul them back to him. I got them in yesterday, but I can't keep them corralled too long. It's a fair drive, to Rands, and my CD player is on the blink, and I could use some company...." her voice trailed off.

Jenny's first impulse was to say no. She really did want to spend some time on her computer, but the wistful look on Elsie's face stopped her. That, and the fact that if they went to Rand's ranch, Rand might be there. She would like to see Rand again. The book could wait.

"Sure, okay. I can work on the book later. It's too nice a day to stay inside anyway. Are you ready to go right now?"

"I have to go back home and hook up the trailer and load the cows, I needed to come to town first and mail a check. I didn't want to drag the trailer along."

"Let me change my shoes, and I'll be ready," Jenny said, slipping off her flip-flops and going into the bedroom for socks and tennis shoes. She remembered Elsie's pickup, and didn't want axle grease on her feet.

Elsie chatted on the drive to her ranch. "You need to talk to Gramps. I'm sure he knew who Barney Morgan was, and he's full of stories. He went to

Thermopolis today to visit an old army friend, that's why I'm in charge of the cows."

"I'd like to talk to him and some of the other old people in the area," Jenny said. Until Elsie had suggested talking to her granddad, Jenny hadn't considered oral history, but Elsie was right, it would be a good source of information that the library wouldn't have.

Elsie nodded, turning the pickup into a driveway near a set of corrals that looked as if they were about to fall apart, but somehow held a little group of colorful cows and engaging spotted calves. Jenny had never seen longhorns up close, and was amazed at how colorful they were. Brown and white, black and white, one brown with black stripes, and two large cream-colored ones. The cows all had long, up-sweeping horns. They looked dangerous.

"I'll invite you over to supper some

night. It will be fun," Elsie said. She wheeled the pickup around and backed it up to a goose-neck stock trailer. When she was in the proper place, how she knew Jenny didn't know, she put the pickup in park and jumped out.

"Need any help?" Jenny asked, feeling she had to offer but not exactly knowing what she could do anyway.

"No, I'm fine. I've got this trailer down pat," Elsie said. She did. In less than five minutes she had the trailer hooked up to the pickup and was back inside, driving to the corral and expertly backing up to the rather dilapidated alleyway where the cows were waiting.

Elsie put the pickup back in park and said, "Don't get out. These cows load better than some horses, but they might spook if they don't know you. I'll have them loaded in a minute."

Jenny watched out the rear view mirror. Elise was right.

Once she set the gates, the cows and calves jumped into the trailer as if they did it every day.

When she got the trailer locked up and was back in the pickup, Jenny asked. "Couldn't they hurt you?"

Elsie shrugged. "Maybe. But in spite of the horns, they aren't any more dangerous than any other cow," she shifted into drive and moved the pickup and trailer away from the corrals and down the road.

"Rand handles his cows a lot, they're pretty gentle," Elise said. "I think this bunch of cows comes over here just so they can get a free trailer ride home."

She put the pickup in drive and headed down the road. It was about ten miles to the Logan ranch. Elsie kept up a stream of conversation that made the trip go fast.

Jenny was familiar with the county road, and she saw the ruins of the ghost town as they swept by it, but she had no idea which side road led to Rand's ranch.

The road was just past the ghost town, and Elsie turned off the main road, crossed a cattle guard, and said, "The Logan ranch starts here, pretty much. It's pretty big. About 20 thousand acres." That sounded pretty big to Jenny. The wheat ranch that she had been raised on had been just under a 1000 acres.

They crossed two more cattle guards, and in one pasture Jenny saw a herd of the colorful cattle, many with large sweeping horns like the cows in the trailer.

After driving down the gravel road for several miles, or so it seemed, they came to an cattle guard under a high cross piece with a sign stating this was "Logan Longhorns" with a metal longhorn silhouette hanging down from it.

Compared to Elsie's rather run down looking place, Rand's ranch was

well kept up, with new looking corrals, a
large newly painted red barn, and a white
and green house tucked in a yard full of
trees, and some full-bloom lilac bushes.
There was another small house outside of
the fenced yard, with the maroon Chevy
pickup parked near it. Jenny wondered if
that was Rand's house.

Two small groups of younger steers
were in a fenced pasture near the pole
corral, and a man on a black horse was
riding into the group of cattle, picking
one out, and moving it from one herd to
the other.

The yearling he was cutting out of
the herd turned to run back to its herd-
mates, but the black horse was ready for
the movement, and blocked the yearling's
retreat. Again and again the steer ducked
back and the horse was always there,
always one step ahead of it. Finally, the
steer gave up and ran to the second
group, ducking between two larger

animals.

The man on the horse looked their way and rode over to the fence. Jenny's heart flipped. It was Rand.

He waved to them, rode over to the corral fence, dismounted and causally draped the reins over a rail, tying them in a loose knot.

Elsie jumped out of the pickup and Jenny followed.

"Hey, Elise. Hi. Oh, Jenny, hi. Long time no see." He grinned.

"Right," Jenny said, returning his barter. "A whole, let's see, four hours."

He grinned at her and turned back to Elsie, "What brings you two lovely ladies out to my ranchero today?"

Elsie chuckled, obviously at ease with Rand. Jenny felt a stab of jealously, then reminded herself that they were old friends. "Jeez, Rand, pour a little more honey on, why don't you. What do you want?"

"Well, seeing as how you're here with the trailer in tow, and I recognize old Naugahyde's voice," he said as a deep moooo came from the trailer, "I suspect that I'd need flattery or a bribe to get my cows back."

Elsie laughed again.   "Well, Gramps did say, and I quote, 'Those are good lookin' cows, seeings as how they're longhorns, if they like our pasture so well, we oughta jist keep 'em.' But, as he was gone to Thermopolis today to visit Jack Nelson, I grabbed the trailer and smuggled them home."

Rand laughed.   "Thanks for bringing them back. Believe it or not, I went out early this a.m. and fixed that hole in the fence, so hopefully they'll stay home for awhile."

Listening to their friendly barter, Jenny felt out of place. She wondered if there was something between Elsie and Rand. They were so easy and causal with each other.

She wished she felt more secure around men, especially attractive men like Rand. Rand had been friendly and helpful when her car broke down, but maybe he was like that to everyone. It didn't mean he was necessarily attracted to her.

"Where do you want your cows?" Elsie asked, opening the pickup door and jumping back into the pickup.

"Back up to the alley," Rand said. "We can put them in the corral and I'll put them back out to pasture later."

Jenny walked over the corral, not wanting to be in the way. Elsie expertly backed the stock trailer up to the alleyway, and Rand waved a hand to let her know she was in the right place. When she stopped, Rand opened the trailer door and let the cows and calves into the corral. Elsie shut off the pickup and jumped back out.

Once the gates were shut again Rand looked at Jenny. "If you two aren't in a hurry, Mom should be taking cinnamon rolls out of the oven about now. Want to come in for coffee and rolls."

"Sure," Elsie said. "Your mom has to be the best cinnamon roll baker in the county. She always wins ribbons at the county fair," she said to Jenny as they walked with Rand to the house.

The smells coming from the small kitchen were mouth-watering. The smell of cinnamon, sugar, honey and fresh baked bread swirled around and drifted out the door when Rand opened it and stepped aside to let them enter.

Elise introduced Rand's mother, Betty, who was short and slender with streaks of gray running through her short brown hair.

"Jenny Morgan , nice to meet you," she smiled, and held up floury hands from the pie crust she was rolling out. "I'd shake your hand, but mine are full of flour. I hear you're renting the Duncan place and researching a book about your grandfather. Interesting. You can tell us about it over coffee and rolls. Set some on a plate, Rand," she said, "We'll take them into the living room. The chairs are more comfortable and it's hot in the kitchen. Is you Dad coming in?"

Rand grinned. "I don't know, Mom. He was working on that tractor, but the way he was cussin' it, I decided to stay out of the way."

Jenny followed Rand, Elsie and Betty into the large living room, with a coal heating stove in one corner, and two large, colorful quilts hanging on the wall. Quilts also covered the couch and one chair.

Jenny turned to Betty. "Rand told me you are a quilter. These are beautiful."

129

"Why, thank you. I enjoy my quilts," she said, and turned as the kitchen door opened behind her. Rand, standing behind Jenny, whispered, "We've got one on every bed."

"You hush," Betty said. "They are warm in the winter."

Waylyn, tall, arrow straight with a slouch felt hat showing grease stains and a long weathered face, came in. Waylyn had to be well over 6 feet, and Betty would barely reach 5'5". His face showed no sign of temper, and he greeted Elsie with a quip.

"Saw old Naugahyde in the corral. You gotta get out more and fix them fences, girl."

"It's half yours," Elsie retorted with a grin. "Besides, I've seen those longhorns jump your corral fences, and I suspect we'd need six foot high fences to really keep them out."

Waylyn rubbed his chin. "Could be.

They do like to jump." He took the cup of coffee Betty handed him, and looked questioningly at Jenny.

Wolf's rugged good looks must have skipped some generations, Waylyn looked nothing like Wolf or Rand.

Rand introduced them. "Nice to meet you," Waylyn said. "I hear you're researching a book."

Jenny was getting used to everyone in the area knowing what she was doing, and in a way it helped. It saved a lot of explaining on her part.

"She wants to know about Wolf," Rand said.

"Wish I could help," Waylyn said, taking a sip of his coffee. "I never really knew much about him. I don't think grandpa did either. His homestead, what's left of it, is out in the back hills. The cabin burned down back in the 1890s or sometime. Now it's just a hole in the ground. He died when grandpa was, oh, about 6 or 7. 'Bout all I know is that he was a bounty hunter and the legend is he was killed by some outlaw he was trackin'"

Waylyn bit into a roll, and Jenny finished hers, and then took another sip of the strong, hot coffee. Too strong for her taste, but she wasn't about to complain. She felt comfortable here in the warm, friendly kitchen, eating the delicious cinnamon rolls. She could understand how Betty won blue ribbons on her baking.

"Wasn't great-grandpop a preacher?" Rand asked.

Waylyn nodded and washed down his bite of roll with drink of coffee. Betty, having put her cherry pie in the oven, joined them.

"He was a circuit riding preacher," Waylyn nodded. "He traveled all through this area, preaching hellfire and brimstone," his light blue eyes twinkled.

132

"I guess he converted a lot of people. Scared 'em to death, or to eternal life, however you want to see it."

"How did that happen?" Jenny asked. The son of a bounty hunter seemed a far stretch to become a preacher.

"Not really sure," Waylyn said, finishing his roll and draining his coffee cup. "Wolf died when Phelan was young, and his raising was taken over by two maiden aunts, and they were very strait-laced, church going women. I guess that influenced him a lot. That's about all I know, Jenny."

"Everything helps, thanks," Jenny said.

Waylyn turned to Rand, who had finished his sweet roll and was aimlessly chasing stray crumbs around on his plate with his fork.

"Are the horses in?" Waylyn asked.

"Yeah, I brought them in when I got in Raven to ride out and fix that hole in the fence. I wanted get in a little cutting practice while we had those calves up."

"Why don't you saddle up one of those youngsters and we can take these Houdini cows back and check the late calvers. Add your fence pliers and bring a sack of staples, we'll check that rough draw and make sure that fence is up."

"Sure. Well, the boss has spoken. See you later, ladies. Thanks for bringing back the cows, Elsie." He put his cowboy hat on and followed his father out the door. Jenny watched his retreating form in admiration. He did look excellent in jeans, with his lean hips and long legs. The rest of him wasn't too bad either. Lost in her contemplation of Rand, she didn't see the look that Betty and Elsie exchanged, or Elsie's grin.

She almost missed what Betty was saying. "....wanted to hear about your book, but the men did all the talking. Tell me about it."

Jenny gave Betty a short version, feeling that Elsie was ready to leave. "Sounds fascinating," Betty said, as Elsie stood up to leave.

"Just a minute," Betty said, and she divided a pan of cinnamon rolls in half, put them on two paper plates, wrapped tinfoil over the plates, and handed one to each girl.

Jenny was surprised. "Why, thank you, Betty, that's great."

Elsie grinned, "I'd better eat them on the way home, or gramps will shovel them all in. He loves your rolls."

"Tell the old goat to come by and visit sometime," Betty said. "I'll give him some too."

As she walked them to the door she held out a hand to Jenny, "It's nice to meet you, Jenny, Come by anytime. I'd like to hear more about your project, and your genealogy research. Enjoy the rolls, and glad to see you Elsie."

After they got in the pickup and headed down the country road back to town, Jenny said, "They're a nice family. Thanks for inviting me along. I enjoyed it."

"I love Betty she, well, she helped me through a lot at one time. I went to school with Rand, from first grade up to graduation. We went on a few dates, if we were both lonely and there was a good movie, but it was just a friendship kind of thing. No real chemistry. I think we know each other too well. He's kind of like a brother to me."

She grinned, "I think he likes you. He doesn't joke much with women, except me, but then, he thinks of me as a sister," Jenny couldn't tell if Elsie sounded a little disappointed about that fact or not. She hoped that Rand was unattached, but she didn't feel comfortable enough with Elsie yet to ask.

She chose a safer subject. "That's a

good looking horse Rand was riding. It's hard to find a true black horse. But that one is."

"Rand bought him as a colt, and trained him. He left him a stallion and he's been raising some really good foals from him. He hopes to start a line of cutting horses from him. He's won several cutting championships around the area on Raven, and Rand and Dean have won some team penning competitions and team ropings as well."

Elsie grinned. "In fact, Raven's expertise came in handy once. Rand was out riding, and saw these two guys who had poached a nice mulie buck on Rand's land. Well, Rand practically has all those deer named, and he didn't take kindly to anyone poaching them. The one guy saw him and dived for the rifle. Well, Raven never gave him a chance. He got between that guy and his rifle and wouldn't let him get to it. I guess, the way Rand tells it, he did the best bulldogging jump he'd ever done, got the guy around his neck in a 'dogger * hold, threw him on the ground, grabbed the rifle himself, and turned them in to the game and fish. He not only got to mount the trophy head, but he got a $1000 reward. He took the money and bought a really nice broodmare to breed to Raven."

Jenny laughed. "In other words, Raven got a reward as well. A new girlfriend."

Elsie laughed and then fell silent, and Jenny couldn't think of anything to say either, being content to watch the green hillsides roll past, wondering what it would be like to live so far from civilization.

Not that she would get that chance. This was only a summer vacation. Come fall, she would be back into the bustle of

(*a bulldogger hold.)

Billings, running her library and teaching rowdy elementary students.

Still, she had a mental image of herself in Rand's arms, his lips brushing her cheek, and his lean body against hers. Then, suddenly, the image changed, and she was in Wolf Logan's arms. She remembered vividly the dream, Wolf's body, Wolf's kisses.

Rand and Wolf Logan, where did they fit into her life?

Chapter 11
Present

It was late-afternoon by the time Jenny got back to the house, but she didn't consider the trip to Rand's a waste. For one thing, she didn't have to buy breakfast foods for a couple days, Betty's cinnamon rolls were great, and she hoped she could save them until breakfast.

Jenny had enjoyed the trip, and when Elsie dropped her off she said, "Thanks for going with me, I enjoyed our visit. I'd like to get together again."

"Wait just a minute, I forgot to give you my card the other day, it has my phone number. I'll run inside and get one for you."

She got back and handed the card to Elise. "Call me anytime, and thanks for the fun morning."

Elsie took the card and slipped it in the hip pocket of her jeans. "Thanks. I'll do that. Thanks again for going along today, I enjoyed the company."

Jenny had enjoyed it as well. She watched the pickup and trailer disappear down the road, and was glad that Elsie wanted to be her friend. Not only that, but she knew Rand....it definitely would make it easier for Jenny to see him as well, something she wanted to do.

Jenny decided that getting her new life in order for the time being was more important than the book, so she went to the post office, rented a mail box, and filled out a change of address card to send to the post office in Billings.

She also borrowed a phone book from Pat, the post-mistress, and called the Dish people to find out about getting a satellite dish hook-up for the summer. The installer was in the area; he agreed to come by.

Plus, the post office was a the social hub of a small community, and she could get to know her neighbors.

She ate supper at the small cafe that was a part of the general store, the sandwich was homemade and delicious.

The sun was still high. When she got back to the house she turned on her computer and entered the new information into the reference file. She had a lot on Barney, but there was still a lot missing about his wife, Kathy. Basically all Jenny had about her was her name, and the fact that she lived in Wild Rose. There must have been something about her that caused Barney Morgan to be such a supporter of woman's rights, even back then.

A surprise knock on the door proved to be the Dish Network installer. The house had a dish attached. The installer redid the wiring, which was old and weathered, installed the new descrambler box, and, after she gave him her debit care to pay for a three month's subscription, she had television.

Then she settled into her recliner and checked out her new television channels. She found the History Channel, to listen to it as much as watch it, but it did help her research into the old west, and sat down to enter the newest research notes, still wondering about Kathy.

Where could she find the information? More microfiche, maybe. There were some books in the Wyoming History room. Tomorrow she would drive to Red Bluffs and take the entire day researching the books that couldn't be checked out.

When she finished adding the research notes, she created a new file titled 'Dreams' and recorded everything she could remember about the dreams she had in the ghost town. They read like the opening chapters of a western novel.

"I may have something here," Jenny mused as she finished recording the dreams. She wondered what a dream interpreter would say about them. Maybe she could write two books, the book on Barney Morgan and a western novel. She was finding that she enjoyed the writing process. She had written articles for her college paper, maybe being a writer was her calling.

The sun was laying long shadows by the time she finished typing. The unease was coming back. It was a feeling like she once had walking home late from the mall in Billings, and saw a car with several young men in it cruise by slowly, then turn and cruise back. Luckily, a police car turned onto the street, and other car picked up speed and left her, the police car following. She had went into a convenience store and called home, asking her roommate to come and pick her up.

She remembered that feeling now, the fast heart rate, and the cold feeling in the pit of her stomach.

Moving like a sleep walker, she left the kitchen and went into the bedroom for her tennis shoes. She saw the tangle of turquoise stones on her dresser. They seemed to glow in the dim light, and Jenny picked them up and put them around her neck. They felt cold as ice on her bare skin.

It was the call again, the call of Wild Rose. It was time to go.

Chapter 12
1885

Jen was standing on the porch of her house, her calico skirt swirling around her ankles. The wind sent dust devils spinning down the road, but the dust was not what she was watching. Her eyes were watching for a lone rider.

The town bustled around her in the early evening light, she could hear the creak of a wagon, the snap of a freighters whip, and the faint sound of piano music from the saloon. Dimly she was aware of horses trotting up the main street to swing up to the hitch rail by the saloon, and couples walking along the boardwalk. But these were secondary sights and sounds. She knew that Wolf was coming, coming soon.

Then, far away in the distance, she saw a dark speck, growing larger as it came nearer. A rangy black horse, walking slowly, carrying his burden gently. Taking the road step by careful step. Something was wrong. Black Eagle seldom walked. He was too nervous, too high strung. If he walked it was lightly, almost dancing, restrained by his rider from breaking into a faster pace. Now, he was walking slowly and carefully, taking care of the man who, Jen could see as they neared her, was barely conscious.

She picked up her skirts and ran towards them, then slowed her pace. Black Eagle would undoubtedly spook if she charged him. Heart pounding, she walked towards the horse, talking to him softly, reaching out her hand towards his white-striped nose. "Nice boy, easy, Black Eagle. Easy."

Sensing a friend, Black Eagle whinnied and reached out his nose to touch her hand, as if glad that there was a human there to help. She took the reins and made sure she had a tight grip on the horse before she looked up to the man slumped in the saddle. She was afraid he was dead.

He felt the horse stop, and tried to straighten in the saddle. "Almost there," he said, the words barely more than a whisper. "Just a little farther, boy, and we'll be there." Black Eagle jerked the reins from Jen's hand as Wolf touched him lightly with his spur.

The horse knew the way, and Jen walked beside Wolf, ready to catch him if he lost consciousness and fell. She saw the dark purple stain on the back of his shirt, and felt the fever when she gripped his hand.

"Bushwhacked. Should have been watching.   Damn   woman   stealer. Probably killed her. Took my woman. Bushwhacker. Woman stealer."

The   disjointed   phases   meant nothing to Jen. She wondered who was he talking about, but put the question out of her mind.   Her first concern was getting Wolf back to her house, and tend to the wound.

Black Eagle stopped at her porch. Wolf straightened in the saddle, but Jen could tell the movement pained him.

"You're home," she said. "I'm here. We have to get you inside."

Wolf nodded, and, awkwardly, with no trace of his old grace, pulled his leg over the saddle and nearly collapsed against Jen as his feet hit the ground.

Jen sagged against his weight, but

she knew if he fell she couldn't begin to lift him off the ground. It was hard enough with him sagging against her, his weight was almost too much for her to carry.

"Just a little more, then you'll be in bed," Jen begged. Jen could feel Wolf's control, felt the slack muscles tighten under his shirt. His mouth set in a grim line, leaning heavily against Jen, he slowly moved up the three steps, across the porch and into the house.

Once inside, his strength gave way and he collapsed on the kitchen floor in a dead faint.

Jen lit a lamp and brought it over beside Wolf. The back of his shirt was covered with dried, matted blood, and wet where the wound had reopened.

She wondered if the attackers had followed Wolf, if so, his black horse was a dead giveaway. She hated to leave him, but she felt it was important to make sure

that no one knew he was here. It had to
be done.

Gathering up her skirts, she went
back outside, looking up and down the
dirt track, but didn't see any riders
following. Black Eagle was well trained,
and he would stand ground-tied until
someone picked up the reins. Jen took
the reins and led him around back to the
small shed and corral. She un-tacked the
horse, threw him an arm full of hay from
the pile near the corral and checked the
water in the tank. Black Eagle fell to
eating hungrily, and Jen hurried back to
Wolf.

Wolf still lay as he had fallen, on
his right side. Jen knelt down beside him
and carefully undid the deer horn buttons
and worked Wolf's arm out of his shirt.
But, the shirt was stuck to the wound
with the dried blood; Jen was afraid to
pull it off and start the bleeding again.
She could see the edge of the wound, red

and swollen and purple, and smell the blood.

Wolf was muttering again. "Mollie. Damn it. Arizona took her. Burned the cabin. Couldn't put it out. Too far gone. Damn bushwhacker. Woman stealer. Outlaw."

Jen dipped warm water from the reservoir on the coal stove, and carefully poured it on the shirt to soften the blood so she could remove it. Finally the buckskin, slippery with water and blood, peeled off the wound.

One look told Jen she needed someone with more knowledge. The wound was deep, and there was a greenish-yellow discharge oozing of it. Swallowing her sickness, Jen looked away.

Wolf was still unconscious, and Jen thanked whatever caused the sleep. He still breathed so she knew he was alive. She hated to leave him again, but again, she had too. Dr. Alex only lived a few doors down, and Jen hurried down the street to the doctor's house.

She knocked on the door, and a young Sioux Indian woman opened it. "Maria. I need Dr. Alex. Is he here?"

"Jen.   No, he had to ride to the Colonel's ranch. One cowhand, a horse fell on him."

"It's Wolf. He's badly wounded."

"I will come. I know my husband's healing magic as well as the magic from my people. Wait."

She went into a small room off the kitchen, and Jen waited while Maria gathered up bandages, medicines and some healing herbs. Maria's herbs and poultices were as good, maybe even better, than Dr. Alex's white man's medicines.

"This is very bad. Very bad," Maria said, back in Jen's house as she bent over Wolf. "The bullet went very deep, and is still in his shoulder. It has to come out, or he will get sickness in his blood."

"Alex has a long, narrow," she made a motion with her thumb and forefinger. "I will go find them. With that, we can find the bullet." She handed Jen some herbs. "Crush these and mix them with warm water. They will help to cure the sickness."

Jen did as Marie instructed, and soon Marie was back. Maria poked the tweezers into the ragged wound. "Thank the spirits that he is in a deep sleep. We can work without the worry of paining him."

Jen watched, flinching as Maria poked and dug at the wound. Even though Wolf was unconscious, he began to mutter and thrash around as Maria dug for the tiny piece of lead. "Jen, hold him. I think, yes, there it is,"

Jen held Wolf's head and pinned down his arm as he tried to move it.

"Easy, easy," she said, talking to him as if he were an injured child. She gently stroked his neck and back, hoping he could know that she was with him.

Maria got a good grip on the tweezers and pulled. Jen could see the bloody piece of bullet that Maria taken out.

"I have it. He will heal now. I have brought some more healing plants," she took the plants and ground them up on the table. They released a pungent but not unpleasant scent. She wrapped them in the thin cloth and lay it on the wound. "Keep it clean, and put this on again tomorrow. I will bring you more. If he wakes, give him some broth. It will built up his strength. When Alex comes home, I will let him know and he will come."

"Can we move him? The men who wounded him might have followed him here, and we can't risk them finding him."

"Moving him now could be dangerous," Maria said.

"I know. But staying here could be worse. At least he might have a better chance if he isn't here. But we may not have much time."

"I know of a place," Maria said. "It is a cave, often used by my people for vision quests and for hunters a long ways from camp. It is guarded by the spirits of the old ones, and Wolf will be safe there."

"How far?"

"About an hour. High in the hills."

"Then we had best get started," Jen said, gathering up the bloody rags that Maria used to staunch the bleeding and clean the wound, then gathering some food, a canteen, and a blanket.

"I'll get the horses," Maria said, and vanished out the door.

Jen tried to wake Wolf, hoping he could ride upright instead of being tied across the saddle, but the fatigue and the blood loss brought Wolf to the point of complete collapse, and his knees kept buckling and his head fell to the side.

When Marie returned, they half-carried, half-drug Wolf's limp body outside and managed to push and pull him unto the saddle. To Jen's surprise, Black Eagle stood like a rock, as if he, too, knew the urgency of their task.

Jen tied his hands and feet to the stirrups to keep Wolf from sliding off the horse. Once Wolf's body was secured and covered with a blanket, Jen mounted her gentle roan mare, Marie handed her Black Eagle's reins and mounted her own sorrel.

Jen was glad for the early evening shadows, they could hide in the near-darkness. They went at a slow walk, keeping to the back alleys of the town until they were free of prying eyes, then they turned back to the wagon track, with Maria leading the way. Black Eagle, for all his spirit, seemed to sense the necessity of being slow and gentle, and walked as if he were carrying something very young and fragile.

Moving at a slow walk, to jar Wolf as little as possible, the journey took nearly two hours. Finally Maria pointed to a barley visible trail up a steep hillside, and urged her horse forward up the hill.

Jen was glad of the darkness as they left town, but was grateful when the full moon rose, illuminating the unfamiliar surroundings.

The trail was damp from a recent high country rain, and Jen's horse slipped and slithered on the slimy rocks, but she was glad it was rocky. The evidence of their passing would be less noticeable. Plus, they had ridden on a trail that was covered with pine needles, and the horses hooves would not leave a track in the soft mat.

She followed Maria higher and higher, her arm aching from holding

Black Eagles reins. Finally, Maria turned
her horse off the trail onto a narrow
ledge, barely large enough for the three
horses.

A screen of brambles and
chokecherry bushes hid the entrance of
the cave, and Maria pushed them aside so
Jen could enter. The chamber was dry and
cool, and larger than Jen expected. In one
corner was a small hole in the rocks
where smoke from a fire could be drawn
out, and would disappear in the
overgrowth of branches.

It was a perfect hiding place for a
wounded man, but as they unrolled the
bedroll and spread it out on the cave
floor, Jen was terribly afraid that it might
not be needed. She was afraid that Wolf
was dead.

Together, they untied him and to
her relief they could hear his harsh
breathing, so they knew he lived. They
struggled to carry him into the cave, and

then laid him on the blanket. "We should have cut some pine boughs. The bed would have been softer," Maria said.

"It will have to do," Jen said, touching Wolf's forehead. It was burning with fever. She was glad he was still unconscious, but she feared again that he might never wake.

"Where can I hide the horses, and is there a spring nearby?"

"There is a spring, and a small meadow to tie the horses. Perhaps it would be better if you went back to town, as least for the day. Will people not wonder where you are?"

"If anyone asks, I went on a horseback ride. You saw me ride away, but you have no idea where I was going."

"If anyone asks," Maria said. "Tomorrow, I will bring Alex back. We will take care so as not to be seen."

They picketed the horses in the small meadow, and Jen filled Wolf's canteen with water from the spring, and watched Maria ride away before she returned to the cave.

It was very quiet. Even the birds seemed to be mute. All she could hear in the cave was Wolf's harsh breathing, but at least it meant that he was still alive.

Looking around the small room, Jen saw several images pecked in the rock. Indian rock art, creatures and men with horned hats and large, spread fingered hands. It was like looking at a gallery of paintings. Taking a branch from the fire as a torch, Jen walked back into the cave, lighting up the strange drawings, feeling as if she were being touched by the spirits of the old ones, and her brief fright was replaced by a comfortable feeling of being protected. Protected by spirits, as Maria has said. She returned to Wolf's side, suddenly feeling assured that he would survive.

Chapter 13
Present

Sunlight flooded the car. Jenny blinked, and the ghost town came into view, the saloon, still standing. Two other vacant buildings. Not much left of the bustling town she had been a part of all night.

She knew, now, why her house had a familiar feel to it the day she moved in. Rand had said that some of the houses from Wild Rose had been moved to

Crystal Creek. Now she knew that the spirits had led her to the exact house that appeared in her dreams.

For three nights in a row she had been in the ghost town, and had seen visions of the past. She was sure, now, that the experiences were not dreams in the usual sense. She was being given a glimpse into the past, but why? And whose past? Hers? There she wasn't sure.

The thoughts swirled around in her head as she turned the key in the ignition. The SUV started without a hitch.

Jenny glanced down at her hands. Around and under the fingernails on her right hand was a red-brown stain. She examined them closer. What had she done that would leave a stain on her fingers? She never left the car. She had done nothing, except....except for doctoring a wounded man, and washing the blood off the bullet wound. Shakily, she put the Explorer in gear. She wanted to get home before anyone came along. It would be difficult to explain why she spent the night here with a perfectly working car, and blood on her hands.

This time there was no early morning rancher out on an errand. She met no one on the drive back to Crystal Creek, and breathed a sigh of relief when she turned the car into her drive.

Inside the house Jenny went into the bathroom and examined her face in the mirror. There was no other evidence of the dream, and she scrubbed her hands for longer than the 30 seconds that the doctors advised, using a nail brush to get under the fingernails. The blood came off, leaving a rusty stain in the water as she watched it drain away down the sink.

She felt slightly sick. Was it really Wolf's blood that had traveled across time? No way. She checked her hands again, but there was no new blood welling up. She even went outside and checked the Explorer to see if there was anything that she might have scratched herself on. Nothing.

Now she rather wished she hadn't washed it down the drain. Couldn't science these days find out a lot from DNA? Blood would have been a good place to find out if the Wolf in her dreams was indeed Rand's ancestor, but it was too late now.

A siren wailed, and Jenny saw an ambulance rush down the street. She wondered idly where it was going, but since she knew almost no one in town, wherever it was going was no concern of hers.

It would be a good day to do some more research. She remembered seeing a sign, "Crystal Creek Community Library" maybe they would have history local to this area. Maybe she could find some more mention of Kathy Sanders, or Jen, if either of them lived in the area. Since Wolf and Jesse Arizona were real, Jen had probably lived near here as well. Maybe Jenny could find something about her in the library.

The town was small, so Jenny decided to walk; if she checked out too many books she could always walk back and get her car. It was a dry, sunny day, and she felt the need of fresh air.

There wasn't much to the town. All the businesses, with the exception of the K-12 school, were located on Main Street. General store, convenience store, post office, the cafe/bar/dance hall, library, and a small beauty saloon, which advised potential customers that the hairdresser was only there on Monday and Friday, with a number to call for an appointment.

The rest of the town was mainly residential, and there were few people around. Maybe a lot of them worked during the day in Red Bluffs. The library was small and cluttered, books lined the shelves, sat on top of the shelves, and spilled over unto the card catalog. The librarian, a young blond man, rose when Jenny came in. He looked bored, and greeted her with a wide smile.

"Hello, can I help you?" His eyes passed over Jenny appreciatively. "New in town or just passing through?"

"Here for the summer. I'm Jenny Morgan. I'm researching a book on my great-great-grandfather, Barney Morgan, a judge and state senator in the 1890s. He lived in Wild Rose."

"Really. Sounds fascinating. Oh," He wiped his hand on his jeans and held it out to Jenny. "I'm Larry McDaniels. Nice to meet you." Jenny offered her hand and he shook it with enthusiasm.

"I've never heard the name, but there are a lot of books on this area that probably aren't in the main library. I think they have some books written by

167

local people, and some oral histories. What years?"

"The 1880's. He lived in this area from 1882-1890. He proved up on his homestead on what is now the Logan ranch."

Larry came out from behind the curved desk, led the way across the small library and pointed out the Wyoming history section.

"These are some books that might help you," he said, pulling out two large tomes from the bottom shelves. "One is on early day ranching families around the county, and one is specific to this area."

The phone rang and Larry went to answer it.

Jenny took the books to one of the empty tables and checked the index for the names, Sanders and Morgan. Barney Morgan was referenced several times, as sheriff and judge, but no article about him per se. And nothing about Kathy

Sanders at all. A blank.

The only thing that the book confirmed was the location of the old Morgan homestead. At least she had photos of the right ruins.

As she flipped through the book, one picture caught her eye, and she stared at it for a long moment. It was a photo of a dark-haired young woman, holding the reins of a dark-colored horse. "Lorrie J. Carlise, age 18 on her family's homestead," the caption said. That was all. The name Carlise in the index only had one page number, the page with the photo. Nothing more. The name meant nothing, and the brief flash of recognition that she had first felt with the photo was gone.

She shrugged and looked up the Logan family. There was a long story about the present day ranch, mentioning how Wolf homesteaded the land, how Phelan and later his son, JR, took it over and then added on to it through the years of drought and depression, buying out the neighboring ranchers to build a large cattle ranch that was now 100 years old. There was a picture of Rand and Waylyn, posing with a couple of their champion longhorn cattle.

There was one photo of Wolf, standing next to a blond woman holding a baby in a long christening dress that was common in the 1800s. "Wolf, Molly and Phelan, 6-months old," the caption read. There was little else about Wolf, he was mentioned briefly as Phelan's father, a bounty hunter, then the story went on to describe Phelan's narratives of his circuit riding preacher days, how many miles he rode between towns, and how many people he converted.

Someone was impressed by his chosen profession. The two aunts that raise Phelan were featured, with photos and a narrative about how they undertook the raising of a young boy, and did a fine job making sure he was a credit to their family. Wolf's name was almost never mentioned as Phelan's father. Molly, the woman in the photo, wasn't mentioned at all.

It was a lot less than she had heard from Rand.

She still wondered about the photo and went into the index and found it again, looking at it, trying to find the flash of something again. Recognition? She wasn't sure. She took the book to the desk, asking Larry if had a photocopier. "I do. I keep it behind the counter. What you need?"

"Just this photo." Jenny said, handing the book across the counter.

"How much?" Jenny asked as Larry passed back the book and the copy.

"Nah, don't worry about it."

"Thanks," Jenny said, taking the book to re-shelve it. The door swung open, letting in sunlight and tall, stooped woman with short, iron-gray hair.

"Hey, Flora, what's going on?"

"Not much with me, but did you hear what happened to Rand Logan?"

"Rand? No."

"Got bucked off one of those colts he was training. He hit the corral fence, splinted the top rail, and took a wood splinter in his shoulder."

Jenny's head jerked up at Rand's name.

"I heard the ambulance," Larry said. "Wondered where it was going. Sounds like he got bunged up pretty bad," his voice sounded worried.

"Sounded like it. Blackie heard it on the scanner. The ambulance people were saying he may have punctured a lung."

Jenny moved closer to the desk. "How did it happen?"

Flora turned to her, only then

172

noticing another person in the library. "Oh, hi. Didn't see you there. You must be that new gal in town. Renting the old Duncan place."

Jenny smiled. Everyone in town seemed to know who she was and what she was doing. "That's me. I've been to the Logan ranch and I know Rand."

Flora nodded. "He likes to ride them broncs, and I guess one was too much for him. 'Bout all I know. He's gonna get killed one day. Fool kid."

"People do," Larry agreed. "But Rand usually doesn't take foolish chances."

Flora's strident voice jumped in, "There's been a lot of accidents this year. That guy got hit by a train 'tween here and Rocky Point, that girl rolling her pickup, and now Rand."

Larry nodded. "Well, I've heard trouble comes in threes, so it should be over by now, Flora."

"You're right. Do you have any new Sci-Fi?"

Larry reached under the counter, and pulled out two hard backed books with fantastic creatures on the covers. "I thought of you when the main library sent these down."

Larry took the books, did some quick work on the computer, and handed them to Flora.

"Thanks, Larry, these look good." Flora said, taking the books and walking out.

Flora's comment gave Jenny a lot to think about. Rand got hurt in the shoulder, and Wolf had been shot in the shoulder. Blood under her fingernails.... It was getting rather eerie, the way the past seemed to be affecting the present.

"Damn," Jenny muttered, then gave an apologetic smile to Larry, who was looking at her strangely. "It's too bad Rand got hurt, I hope he'll be okay."

"Yeah, I don't know him well, but he's always been friendly to me. I just moved in last year."

Jenny had known that Larry wasn't a native of the area. His hair style, the gold chain around his neck, and his city-style clothes marked him as different.

"Where are you from originally?"

"San Diego. I got tired of the people and the traffic, I think my soul needed less of that and more of nature."

"I guess you came to the right place to get away from people. Why did you choose such a small town?"

"I'm a writer, and two years ago I came to the Red Barn Artist Retreat up the road. I liked the area, then I saw this job. I have a degree in library science, so it was a match made in heaven. I like it. This job is great, its only part time, but pays enough to keep me in groceries, and I get to meet people. In my spare time I'm finishing my first novel, and this a great place to do that."

"Neat. What's it about?"

The phone rang, and Larry said, "Life, what else," before picking up the phone. Jenny picked up her books and lay them on the counter. Larry hung up the phone and took the books.

"I have a card from the Red Bluff's library, is it good here?" Jenny asked, pulling it out of her wallet.

"It works," Larry said, scanning her card and the books.

"Thanks," Jenny said. "I'll see you around."

After she left the library, Jenny thought about Rand. Somehow, things were beginning to make horrible sense. Were she and Rand caught up in some age old drama? Something to do with Wolf and Jen. Who was Jen and how did she figure into Jenny's life? It made sense that Wolf and Rand were psychically connected, they were blood kin. But it would have made more sense for her to be drawn to Kathy Sanders, her great-great-grandmother. Until she could find out more about Kathy, there was still a big piece missing in the Barney Morgan story.

She was restless when she got back to her house. She wanted to go see Rand but wasn't sure if she would be welcome. She had known the family for such a short time. Elsie. Elsie was Rand's friend, and wanted to improve on Jenny's acquaintance. She dialed Henry's number and Elsie answered.

"Oh, God," Elsie said when Jenny told her the news. "No, I hadn't heard, I've been outside in the corral all morning. How bad is it?"

Jenny related all she knew, all that Flora had told Larry. Jenny felt a little awkward but asked anyway. "I'd like to go with you if you go to the hospital."

"I'll be there in a half hour," Elsie

said.

Betty was in the waiting room when Jenny and Elsie arrived at the modern hospital building in Red Bluffs. The ride would have been hair-raising if Jenny hadn't been as anxious as Elsie to get there. She was just glad that the secondary road wasn't a high priority on the Wyoming Highway Patrol's list.

"How's Rand," Elsie asked his mother.

"Elsie, Jenny. Hi. Rand will be find. The wood didn't hit anything vital, and just missed the collar bone. He'll be sore for a few days, and won't be doing any roping, but they only plan to keep him overnight. He can go home tomorrow."

"Can we see him?" Elsie asked

"He's pretty doped up and I hope he's sleeping, but you can peek in," Betty said

Rand was laying on his back, his

face pale against his dark hair. Jenny felt her heart catch in her throat, but she saw Rand's chest rise gently with his breathing. She could see the bandage on his shoulder barely visible under his blue-checked hospital gown.   Jenny wanted to tip-toe in and kiss his cheek, but she wasn't his girlfriend, so she contented herself to watching him sleep for a moment.

Suddenly, it was as if Wolf's harsh features were superimposed over Rand's younger face. Jenny wished Wolf was in this clean, comfortable room, instead of on the hard rock of the cave in the hills. She suddenly wondered if he were still alive. She had to find out.

"Let's go," she said to Elsie.

"Yeah, I've gotta get home anyway, Gramps is going to wonder where I went."

Back in the waiting room, they hugged Betty, who once again assured them that Rand would be okay.

"I thought he gave up riding the broncs," Elsie said.

"He gave up rodeo, but he still likes the challenge of those young horses, and he has a lot of them to train. Normally, he's pretty careful, and these colts are pretty mellow, but they are still colts."

"How did the accident happen," Elsie asked.

"Rand said when he turned the colt, his leg somehow caught in the fence, and the bay spooked. Rand actually bailed off to avoid breaking a leg, but the fence rail split. I saw most of it, and it was a lucky thing I was nearby."

"I'd like to come over tomorrow and visit him again, if that would be okay." Jenny said hesitantly.

"I think he'd appreciate that. He'll be laid up for awhile, and he'll get bored. Thanks. I appreciate both of you coming today."

    "See you later, Betty," Elsie said as she and Jenny walked back to the pickup, each thinking their own thoughts.

    Jenny was thinking about Rand, and Wolf, and how close to the present the dreams were. It was scary in a way, but she felt she had to keep dreaming. It was the only way to find out what would happen to Wolf, and to Jen. She felt she had to keep Wolf alive, maybe even to keep Rand safe. She wasn't sure, but it was how she felt.

Chapter 14
1885

The events of the previous night and the day had worn Jenny out. All she wanted to do was watch something mindless on T.V. and go to bed. She did not want to go to the ghost town tonight, but she thought of Wolf, alone in the cave. If she didn't go, would he die? And if he died, would Rand die?

Still, she fought the pull. Fought it as one might fight a tenacious spirit. It was like being sucked into a whirlpool. Jenny felt herself going under, deeper, deeper into the abyss. She walked into the living room, and the mundane sound of the television. She went into the kitchen, and found it changed. An old coal range seemed to be superimposed on the modern stove. The refrigerator looked like an old-fashioned pantry. But things weren't really changed. It was like the modern appliance were overshadowed by transparent versions of the old. Then, Jenny's mind snapped back, and the kitchen was again the modern version.

Back in the living room, Jenny sank down on the couch. The ghost town was bad, but to have the past invade here would be much worse. So far, the dreams hadn't hurt her, and it might not matter where she was. If that was the case, she may as well go back to the ghost town. At least she could leave the dreams there. She wasn't sure what would happen to her in the house.

Once she got behind the wheel of the car, and headed to the Wild Rose, the pull eased. The spirits had their way, and they knew she would continue to the rendezvous point

#######

1885

Jen was standing by her window, looking out over the evening bustle of the town. The same man had been sitting on the porch of the saloon, seemingly asleep, all day. On the other side of the house was another man, sitting in the alley, sipping occasionally on a bottle. Jen knew the two men were not as innocent as they appeared, but that they were watching her should she return to Wolf.

She wasn't too worried. The men had been there all day, and were probably getting bored. By full dark they would be less alert; the one nipping on the bottle might well be drunk by evening.

It was not yet dark enough to light the lamps, but Jen closed the curtains on the small windows, and began her preparations for the evening.

She moved a rocker near the window, stuffed it with a couple of pillows to simulate a human body.

She took the precaution of concealing the Navy colt pistol Wolf had given her in the pocket of her split riding skirt.

She sat away from the other window and watched the man with the bottle. Just as she expected, soon his head lolled, and bottle fell from his hand.

At full dark, Jen slipped out the back door, and keeping to the dark, shadowed alley, she walked carefully to

Marie's house.

"They are watching your house," Marie said, when she answered Jenny's soft knock and ushered her into the house.

"They have been all day. I guess they think I'll lead them to Wolf. But why? The one by the saloon looks like one of the sheriff's men. But why would they be watching me?"

"I don't know. If Alex were here, perhaps he could tell us. He must have been delayed at the ranch. Perhaps the sheriff is protecting you."

"If so, why didn't they come to the house? I have to get back to Wolf, but I don't want to endanger him." She thought a minute.

"Loan me a pair of Alex's pants. If they think I'm just some cowhand heading out of town, they will be less likely to connect him with Wolf."

Marie found her a pair, and even

though they tied them at the waist with a piece of frayed rope, they were still several inches too long; Jen had to roll up the legs to be able to walk. Still, with her hair tucked up under one of Alex's slouch hats and wrapped in an old jacket, she would look like a man from a distance. She transferred the Navy Colt into the pocket of the trousers, making them bag even more with the added weight.

Maria helped her saddle her horse in the barn behind Maria's house, which was sheltered by several other buildings and well hidden from the watchers. Maria wished her well, saying, "I will let you know if anything happens in the town."

Worried about eyes that might be watching her, Jen rode slowly out of town, trying to give the impression of a cowhand heading back to the ranch.

She reached the cave without being followed, as far as she could tell. She tied her horse next to Wolf's in the thicket below the cave. She was terribly afraid of what she might find.

In spite of the fact that the man's pants kept wanting to slither off her hips and unroll at legs, Jen made her way to the cave.

Wolf was awake, and for one breathless moment Jen found herself staring into the barrel of his pistol.

"It's me," she said, carefully reaching up and pulling the man's hat off her head and letting her brown hair tumble down over her shoulders. Wolf had raised himself on one elbow, now he lay back down and lowered the gun.

He looked her up and down. "Why the get up?"

Jen set down the bundle that she had packed before leaving. It had coffee, food, clean rags and medicines that Maria supplied. The cave was warm, even though the fire had died down to coals.

There was wood stacked inside the cave, and now she rekindled the fire before she answered Wolf's question.

"Someone was watching the house. I slipped out dressed in Dr. Alex's old clothes." She glanced down ruefully. "They are a little big."

Wolf grinned. "Just a little."

Jen was so glad to find Wolf alive and obviously on his way to healing that she felt giddy. She brushed the hair out of her eyes and busied herself with the supplies. She found the small pot she had packed to make stew in, and the coffee pot. "I've brought food. I'm going down to the spring to get water, then I'll make coffee and fix up something to eat. I expect you're hungry."

Wolf grinned. "Now that you mentioned it, I am. Coffee would be good too."

"I'll have it ready in a minute."

She returned with the water, and

put the coffee pot on to boil. Then she sat down beside Wolf.

"Let me look at the wound," she said, easing the shirt off so she could see the injury.

"What happened?" Wolf asked, as he hitched himself out of his shirt to help her. "I woke up here in this God-forsaken cave and wondered how I got here. The last few days are sort of hazy."

Jenny poured the warm water over the rags she had brought and began to wash the wound, which seemed to be healing as well as could be expected. "Your horse brought you to my house. I'm not sure how you managed to stay on. I was afraid whoever did this might be following you. Your tracks lead to my place, so Maria and I hid you here."

"I rather doubt that he would follow. I'm sure he thinks he killed me. That's good, really. Now he won't expect anything else from me."

190

He stared out into space.

"Has Sheriff Campbell been by your place? Wolf asked.

Jen shook her head. "No. He's never liked me, but he usually leaves me alone. Why?"

"Just wondered." Wolf said. He flexed the fingers on his gun hand, and rolled his shoulder, working the stiffness out, but Jen could see the grimace on his face as the pain hit.

"You can't rush the healing," Jen said. "You have to take it easy for awhile."

"I can't." Wolf said. "Something big is going to happen soon in Wild Rose. I have to prevent it."

"You're in no shape to prevent anything right now," Jen snapped. "Whatever it is, let the law handle it."

Wolf looked at Jen for a long moment, and Jen wondered what was going on in his mind. The silence was so deep that she could hear the sound of the breeze barely stirring the leaves of the bushes outside.

"There is a shipment to the territorial governor from an English Earl, an antique jewel encrusted silver candelabra. The jewels have unlimited value, especially if they are taken out of the candelabra and sold off individually. They would be difficult to trace if pieced out and sold one at a time throughout the territory."

The water was boiling on the fire. Jen left Wolf and made the coffee, poured Wolf a cup before returning to re-bandage the wound.

Wolf took a long drink of coffee and continued, "We can't afford for these to fall into Arizona's hands. The Earl is a powerful man, and it wouldn't do to upset him. The man who was at your house last week is a federal judge. He promised the Earl that the shipment would arrive safely. He wants me to make sure that Arizona doesn't rob this stage."

"Why you? Tell Sheriff Campbell and let him handle it. You've lost a lot of blood, and you're in no shape to take on anyone, especially Arizona, or whoever it was that shot you in the first place. Let me get the Sheriff."

Jen finished rebandaging the wound, glad to see there was no infection. She began gathering up the bloodied rags and stuffing them in the saddle bags.

Wolf grabbed her arm, squeezing it so hard that Jen let out a startled "Ouch."

"Sorry. But you can't go to Campbell. The judge and I suspect that Campbell is the one who's been giving Arizona the schedule of the stages that have gold shipments and treasures on board. Twice he's had Arizona in custody and twice Arizona has escaped."

"The Sheriff?" Jen asked,

incredulous.

"Yeah," Wolf said bitterly. "A sweet setup, don't you agree?" He took his gun and idly twirled the cylinder. The clicking of it grated on Jen's nerves.

To take her mind off the sound, she took the pan she had packed and began cooking some bacon. Inside the pack she had cold biscuits as well. That would do for breakfast.

"If you're right, it is. But how can you prove it?" She asked.

"If Campbell knows about these jewels, he'll get word to Arizona, and they will surely rob this stage. The judge and I have been working on getting rid of Arizona and getting Campbell taken down from his position of sheriff. But we need proof. This could be our chance to get that proof. "

He paused to take a sip of the hot, strong coffee.

"As far as we know, no one else

knows that the shipment is on this stage. We arranged for Campbell to get the information. If Arizona tries to rob the stage, it will be the proof we need, and we hope to convince Arizona to talk. We need to prove Campbell's part in this, but so far he's protected by his tin star."

Jen was almost afraid to ask the next question, but it had been nagging her. "When you were hurt, you were muttering something about '...he killed her.' Who shot you and who did he kill?"

In the firelight, Wolf's eyes glittered savagely. "I don't remember saying anything."

"It was Arizona, wasn't it? He shot you. But who did he kill?"

"Don't pry, Jen. This is none of you concern."

"Aren't you afraid that whoever shot you might be back, might try to finish the job? If you keep on with this business it won't be long before Arizona

or someone else has better aim." In her
fear for Wolf, Jen forgot everything else,
she was trying to convince him to live.
"Forget Arizona. Especially if he thinks
you're dead. Whatever he did is in the
past. We can leave, find a ranch
somewhere. Please," The last word was
almost a whisper. She didn't want Wolf
to know how much she cared.

Wolf's face hardened. "Not until I
finish this. You don't know the whole
story, Jen, so don't push me. I'll tell you
about it some day, but not now. The less
you know, the safer you are."

"I don't care. Tell me now. I can't
stand your coming and going, wondering
if someday I'll see you brought in across a
saddle. What's the point?"

Wolf's eyes glittered fiercely.
"Anytime you want to go, Jen, go. But I
have to finish this job. The judge is
counting on me, and I ain't giving it up.
I can't stop until I get Campbell and

Arizona. So, stay or go, it's your choice.
Where's my horse?"

"Picketed below the cave. But you
can't go into town. They will be waiting
for you."

"That's what they expect. I plan to
beat them to Red Hills Crossing. Its the
best place for an ambush, and that's
where they'll be. They won't expect me
there."

"I'm going too," Jen said, following
Wolf's progress through the spiny
chokecherry bushes and feeling the sharp
twigs scratch her face and pluck at her
shirt sleeves.

"For God's sake, Jen. I can't catch
these guys if you're with me."

"I can't go back to town. What if
they're watching my house?"

Wolf paused a minute. "Okay, you
have a point, but you'll have to keep up."

Wolf saddled his horse and swung
into the saddle. The pace he sat was fast,

and had Jen been less resolved to go with him she would have given up. She had no idea where she was and she had to push her mare hard to keep Wolf's black horse in sight. Suddenly, he pulled up the black and dismounted, motioning Jen to do the same.

"Quiet," he said softly. They tied the horses to the stout bushes and slipped through the trees. Now Jen could hear the mutter of human voices.

She could smell wood smoke, and as Wolf parted the bushes she saw the eye of a small campfire. Around it were three men, Sheriff Campbell, a young red-haired man and one that had the long, black hair and darker skin of an Indian.

Of the three of them, the red-haired man, who she knew must be Jesse Arizona, had the softer features. He looked almost boyish, especially compared to Sheriff Campbell's harsh, florid features. The Indian's face was impassive, but the crooked nose and thin lips gave him an evil look.

"The stage will pull out of Rocky Point at 8 a.m. tomorrow," Sheriff Campbell said. "Should put it here about 3 or 4 p.m. The jewels are on this stage."

"Once we get the jewels, how in the hell do you plan for us to peddle them. Everyone in the country knows what they are," Arizona said.

"Leave that to me. I have a contact who will pay well for them."

"What's the cut?" The Indian man asked.

"Bill Blackstone. A renegade Ute," Wolf said softly. "Well, a half breed. Father was a trapper. Hates most whites."

"About $20,000 each," Campbell said.

Jen was stunned. She had no idea the jewels were that valuable. No wonder they were bent on stealing them and Wolf was set on protecting them. She wondered where they planned to sell the jewels.

"What about Logan," Arizona asked. "Are you sure you took care of him?"

"Don't worry about Logan. He's either dead or near dead. My men are watching his woman's house. If he's alive, and if he contacted her, she'll lead us to him."

"You mean you didn't make sure he was dead? Hell, Campbell, he could botch this whole thing. You find him. Today. Make sure you finish the job."

Beside her, Jen felt Wolf's start of suprise. He hadn't known who shot him, he hadn't known it was Campbell.

Arizona's face was no longer pleasant. Now Jen could see the killer surfacing in the rounded boyish planes, and even the sheriff cringed away from him.

"All right," the Sheriff Cambell

sounded like a sulky little boy caught doing something wrong. "I'll find him and make sure he's dead. I want him as bad as you do."

"I'm sure. If he catches up to you, fine upholder of the law that you are, he'll make and example out of you, hang you at midday in the town plaza."

"That would be a new experience, sheriff. Lookin' at the bars from th' other side." The dark haired man said, grinning maliciously.

The sheriff gave him a sour look. "You'd be right there beside me, Breed."

"Don't bother me none, I've been there afore."

Wolf motioned to Jen and they slipped back to the horses.

"So Campbell is part of the gang," Jen said. "Does anyone else in Wild Rose know?"

"I doubt if anyone else cares much. Arizona leaves the town alone, and most of the town people don't ride the stage."

"What are we going to do now?" Jen asked as Wolf gave her a hand up on her horse.

"I'm going to get Campbell. He'll think he's seeing a ghost. Once I take him in, then I'm going after Arizona." He looked at Jen, and she could see some struggle going on in his mind.

"I need you to do something, Jen. I need you to ride to Red Bluffs and send a telegram to Judge Barney Morgan, he's staying at the Royal Hotel in Rocky Point. Don't telegraph from Wild Rose. Tell him I have the proof we need, and to get here as soon as he can. Tell him to stop the stage, or at least get the jewels off. Here's some money for the telegraph and, if you want, a hotel room." He dropped three silver dollars into Jen's hand.

"I think it will be safe for you to go home, I doubt they will try anything in the town, too many people around. Just

202

be careful riding back. I don't want to worry about you being in Arizona's hands."

He swung on the black, then grabbed the rein of Jen's horse, pulled it alongside him, and leaned over and gave Jen a quick kiss. "Be careful, keep to the trails, and ride fast. You look like a man in those clothes. That's good. Now, get going. You need to be in Red Bluffs by daylight."

With that, he let go of the horse's reins and slapped the mare on the haunches. The mare jumped ahead, Jen grabbed the saddle horn to regain her balance. Wolf reined the black around and melted into the warm darkness.

Jen heard the hoof beats fade into the distance, and wondered if she would ever see Wolf again.

How could he fight Arizona and Sheriff Campbell with a wound in his shoulder? Could he even shoot? There was nothing she could to do protect him now, except going to Rocky Point and telegraph Barney Morgan, and hope he could reach Wild Rose in time. Jen dug her heels into the mare's side, and galloped down the trail.

Chapter 15
Present

Jenny Morgan woke with a jerk. Her hair was damp with sweat, and her legs ached. The insides of her knees felt like they were rubbed raw, as if by saddle leather.

"Whew," Jenny muttered. "Wow!"

She lay back on the seat, watching the early morning shadows shorten as the sun rode higher. The dream had been almost too pat. She had been reading about Sheriff Campbell, and the writer had hinted that Campbell was slightly crooked, but had given no details.

She also knew that Barney Morgan had been a judge before he ran for the newly organized senate, and in this dream he was a judge, and friend of Wolf Logan's.

Were the dreams only dreams? Products of her subconscious mind, mixing and stirring the research from the day before and bringing it to life? Maybe she had read the names Wolf Logan and Jesse Arizona somewhere, before the dreams began, but she could have sworn she had not.

She decided to get a little ahead of the story by researching some more, and she didn't want to drive to the 45 minutes to Red Bluffs, so she went back to Crystal Creek, stopping by the small convienence store for some packaged donuts and a cup of coffee for breakfast, and then went to the library. The sign said it wasn't open until nine, so Jenny went to the house, parked her car, and then walked back to the library.

Larry was delighted to see her, and has several more books, bristling with markers.

"This library has a lot of local books, many self-published, that no other library has. I was intrigued by your project, and thought it was a good way to learn more about the area for myself. I found several interesting items."

He opened one book, and began reading, "'The rail head at Crystal Creek was, for many years, the only one between Red Bluffs and Rocky Point. Most of the ranchers trailed the cattle to the stockyards here to ship them out on the trains'.... Crystal Creek also had a band of outlaws. Lead by one Jesse Arizona. Love that name. Fascinating." Larry grinned. "Trouble with research, I

207

get sidetracked by interesting byways. What about you?"

Jenny laughed. "I do. I have a whole file of interesting 'stuff' that won't fit in the book."

"Another interesting thing, this is cool. I was reading about Wolf Logan and Rand's family, and I noticed an odd thing. Wolf Logan, Phelan, Wolf's son, Waylyn and Rand, whose full name could be Randolph, all mean Wolf. That's kind of weird, A whole family of wolves." He grinned again. "Do you think maybe they're werewolves?"

Coming from Wild Rose, and the weird dreams, Jenny wouldn't discount anything at this point, but she found it hard to believe that ranchers could be werewolves. More like Indians that named their children after animals.

"I doubt if they are werewolves, I can't imagine cowboy werewolves," Jenny said. "You're sure they all mean

Wolf?"

Larry flipped through a book titled, "Origin of Names."

"See, Phelan is a Celt name, meaning Wolf, and the Wolf was reverenced," he flipped some more pages. "Waylyn means son of Wolf, and Randolph," he flipped backward, "It means Wolf Counsel. I found that very interesting. I wonder if Rand knows?"

Jenny was surprised at the unique way that Wolf's legacy carried over to his descents. Surely Waylyn knew the origins of the name, why else would he name his own son Rand?

Jenny wondered about her own name, she had never been curious about the origin of her name before, but she was now.

The phone rang; when Larry went to answer it Jenny looked up her name, but there was no connection to Kathy, her great-great-grandmother, Mary Barlow, her grandmother, or Marlene, her mother. She shrugged. Sometimes, a name was just a name.

Larry had done a lot of research, and much of it would be interesting tidbits for the book.

"Barney Morgan, federal judge, was in Wild Rose today at the request of one of the town's citizens," It was a copy of a newspaper article that was talking about cleaning up corruption in the town. Further down on the page was another copy from the same newspaper. *"The Trial of Sheriff Campbell,"* was the headline.

"Campbell, the Sheriff of Wild Rose for five years, was tried today on several counts of stage coach robbery, profiteering, and using the power of his badge to cover up his illegal activities. Campbell allegedly worked for several years with members of the infamous Arizona gang, giving them information on

the stage schedule and what stages were carrying shipments of valuables, such as payroll or boxes of gold from the nearby mines. He was brought before Federal Judge Barney Morgan for trial. However, the trial had to be rescheduled, as the chief witness for the prosecution was not in evidence."

Reading it gave Jenny goosebumps. Again confirming the accuracy of her dreams.

Jenny wondered who the chief witness was. Was it Wolf?

She photocopied the pages of the book and added it to her notebook.

Larry finished his phone call, and came back to help her. "Those help?" he asked.

"Very much, thanks. I appreciate you doing that for me."

"No problem. I like research, and it sometimes gets boring here, I should thank you."

Jenny laughed, picked up the books she decided on, and waited while Larry checked them out for her. Then she left the library and went to the post office to check her mail.

Betty Logan was in the post office. She greeted Jenny with a friendly smile. "Hi, Jenny. I'm going to pick up Rand today, he can come home but he has to take it easy for a few days."

"I'm glad he can come home, tell him I asked about him." Jenny said.

Back at the house, Jenny entered the data into her computer, including the newest installment of the dream. "I should write Westerns," she muttered. Indeed, the dreams did read like a novel, with the characters well drawn, lifelike and three dimensional.

Of course, Jenny had the advantage over most novelists, she had interacted with the characters, and knew them more personally, especially Wolf, than most writers knew their fictional creations. She had heard about writers who fell in love with their characters, and she knew that she was falling in love with Wolf. But he wasn't made up. He was a real person. And, to Jenny, he wasn't in the past, but he was alive. As alive as Rand and Elsie.

She finished recording the dream and shut down her computer, thinking about the research she had compiled, and wondered if she really had or would even find enough to make a book, at least a book worth reading.

The ringing of the phone was an interruption that she welcomed as a reprieve from her thoughts and the research. Especially when the voice on the other end made her heart take a wild jump. Rand!

"How would you like to go with me to a roping tomorrow? I can't rope yet, but I've got cabin fever. It won't hurt my shoulder to drive, and it will be fun."

"I'd love to," Jenny said. "What time?"

"I'll pick you up around 7 am., Unless that's to early." Rand was teasing her. Jenny knew she would drag out of bed at 6 to be ready.

"I'll be up," she laughed.

Later that day, as soon as the sun dropped behind the far-off mountain peaks, Jenny didn't wait for the pull, the sickness to descend. She jumped in the car and headed to the ghost town. She wondered wryly if the ghost town had some addictive properties. Now, she was eagerly awaiting the dreams.

Chapter 16
1885

It was barely light when Jen pulled the lathered horse up at the door of the Red Bluff's telegraph office. It was locked up tight. Jen had no idea what time it was scheduled to open. There was a back door, and Jenny pounded on that, hoping that the telegraph operator lived in back of the office.

She pounded again, and heard shuffling footsteps across the floor. The door opened and an older man with graying hair and a growth of bristly whiskers came to the door. "Office is closed. If you need to send a telegram, come back at 9."

He started to shut the door, but Jen pulled the Navy Colt out of her pocket and leveled it on the man. "You will send this telegram right now, or I will shoot you and send it myself."

The man's eyes traveled from the barrel of the Colt up to Jen's face. He read her determination and stepped back. "Okay, lady, okay."

She stepped inside, careful to keep the pistol trained on him while he fumbled with the key to the door that separated the living quarters from the office. "Got robbed once, started locking up afterward," the man said.

The man finally got his equipment ready, and looked at Jen. "You can disperse with the pistol now lady, if you please." Jen noticed that his hands were trembling badly, so she lowered the pistol.

"Thank you. Now, what message do you want me to send and who is it going to?" he asked.

Jen hoped there was someone at the Rocky Point office to take the message.

"This goes to Judge Barney Morgan, at the Royal Hotel in Rocky Point."

"You're in luck, lady, the telegraph office is located in that hotel, so there will be someone on deck, even now. What message did you want sent?"

"Stop the stage. Needed in Wild Rose. Found proof. Going after Arizona. Wolf." Jenny said, having nothing much to do on the wild ride except think about what she wanted to say in the fewest words possible.

"Jeez, lady, you woke me up for that? Couldn't it have waited until a decent time?" But Jenny felt weak with relief when she heard the clicking of the telegraph key.

It was done, so whatever happened the Judge knew that Wolf needed his authority to back him up. She just hoped he would get the message quickly.

"Now," Jen told the telegraph operator, after she paid him for the wire. "I need a horse. Mine's done in. Do you have one I can trade mine for, at least until I come back this way, and then I'll return it."

"Yes ma'm, I've got one you can borrow. Bring him back first chance you get. He's a pretty good horse."

"Fine. Lead the way." Jen followed the man to his stable, leading her horse. He even helped Jen unsaddle Maria's horse and throw the saddle on his tall chestnut.

"Thanks," Jen said. "Now, there's no need for anyone else to know I was here and held you at gunpoint, is there? As you can see, I have friends in high places."

"Yes, ma'm. Just return my horse and I won't say a word to anyone."

Jenny swung up on the chestnut and, keeping to the alleys, because the daylight was creeping in swiftly, rode out of town.

She wanted to get home, take a bath, get out of the scratchy men's clothes, and fall into bed.

She kept the horse at a steady pace, and the distance hills seemed to move no closer as she rode along, but she knew it was a long ride, and she didn't want to push the horse too fast.

She wondered if Barney would be able stop the shipment, and she wondered where Wolf was. Was he trying to trap the outlaws, or had he lost the trail.

She was tired, and she wasn't as

alert as she might have been.

A man came out of a tangle of trees, setting his horse squarely in front of Jen, blocking the road. She reined in, feeling for the pistol in her pants pocket.

She recognized the round-faced man, and the breath caught in her throat. Jesse Arizona!

"Well I'll be damn. Thought you was a man until I saw your face. Planned to rob you, but, now, things might be making sense here. You being a woman, dressed in man's clothes. Campbell said Wolf Logan's woman turned up missing yesterday. You his woman?" He didn't wait for an answer. "Where have you been so early in the mornin'?"

Jen just looked at him, but said nothing.

"Well, well. Nothing to say? But," his eyes scanned the horizon. "This is a dangerous road sometimes. You'd better come with me, for your own protection of course."

He reached over to grab her horse's rein, and Jen pulled the horse away, reaching for her gun, but Arizona, even though he was momentarily off balance, regained it quickly and sat up on his horse, his .45 already in his hand, and pointed straight at Jen.

"I don't like games, miss. Now, you gonna come with me peaceful, or across the saddle. I don't care much either way."

He took her horse's reins and dismounted in one quick motion. Keeping the pistol trained on her, he ran one hand down her trousers and across her hips, impersonally searching her for weapons. He found her pistol and jammed it in his belt, the ran his hands up under her pant legs to the top of her boots, looking for a boot knife.

"Sorry, ma'm. I just figured that Wolf Logan's woman would have a few tricks up her sleeve. If you tell me you don't have a pig sticker in your garter, I'll believe you and not make you take off them pants, but you'd better be telling me the truth."

Jen looked him right in the eye. "I do not carry knives."

"Okay, ma'm. Let's go. We have a stage to catch."

He kicked his horse and Jen's horse was jerked along by the reins.

"You didn't answer my question, ma'm. Why are you out riding so early this morning?"

Jen had had time to think up a lie. "I was looking for Wolf. But I didn't find him. I had to sneak out of the house to keep Campbell's men from following me."

Jesse laughed. "Wolf's dead. All you'll find is a corpse."

Jen sighed in relief. They didn't know Wolf was alive.

She wondered how she could

escape. Jumping off the horse wouldn't work, she couldn't outrun Jesse on foot and she had no doubt he would just shoot her and be done with it if she tried to escape.

The bruising ride seemed to on forever, Jen was just grateful that Jesse hadn't tied her hands. She could hang on to the saddle horn, and she kept a death grip on it for the duration of the ride.

Arizona stopped on a high hill overlooking the stage road, and the man called Breed was waiting for them. Arizona jerked Jen from the saddle. "Tie her up. Good." He told the swarthy man. Breed forced her over to a pile of rocks and tied her hands securely behind her.

"Stage runnin' late," Breed said, looking up at the sun, riding higher in the sky.

"It'll be here," Arizona said. "Campbell back yet?"

"Ain't seen him," Breed said.

Jesse shrugged. "We can do the job without him,"

Jen could hear a rumble in the distance. "Stage coming," Breed said.

The men pulled their kerchiefs up to cover the lower half of their faces, and pulled their hats down low. Arizona tested the ropes around Jen's hands, then he followed Breed down the hill. Jen wondered if Judge Morgan had been able to get the jewels off the stage, but there was nothing more she could do.

It seemed a long time before Arizona came back. When he pulled off his bandana she again saw the killer exposed.

"The stage was empty, no jewels, no passengers, no nothing. Damn it to hell. Wolf had something to do with this, and you're going to tell me."

Jen had several thoughts. She could refuse to say anything, but that might not work in her favor. The jewels were safe, and Wolf, as far as she knew, was still alive, or Arizona would be boasting about killing him.

She wondered if Wolf had captured Campbell, and Arizona didn't know about it. Right now, her only hope was that Wolf and the judge had men out looking for Arizona. They had no idea that Jen was now a prisoner of the gang.

"Well, come on girl. What did Wolf have to do with this. I can assume that Campbell screwed up and didn't kill him after all, and you know where he is." He raised his Colt and gently stroked Jen's face with the barrel. The threat was clear. "Or, Wolf might find you dead across your saddle."

"We heard you talking last night. Wolf knew where you were meeting," she wanted to tell Arizona he must not be as smart as he thought he was, but decided not to push his temper to far. "Wolf must have tipped off someone about the robbery." Jen knew it didn't matter, Arizona would either kill her or he wouldn't.

"That don't make sense, how could Wolf tip off the stage? No way he could get to Rocky Point before it left. No way." He looked at her. "Where were you coming from when I found you?"

Jen didn't say anything, and Jesse grabbed her arm and shook her, causing the rough rope around her hands to scrape painfully.

"Here's what I think. I think you was leaving Red Bluffs, after telling someone what you learned. The telegraph office was closed, so who did you tell."

"The sheriff at Red Bluffs laughed at me," Jen said. "He said not to worry about the stage, there were Pinkertons on it."

"Pinkertons die just like everyone else," Breed said, returning from tying the horses.

"What worries me is where Wolf is. Where is he?" Arizona asked.

"I don't know," Jen said. "He left me last night, I suspect he went after Campbell. Campbell shot him, so he's out for revenge."

"Campbell's wearing a star, Wolf wouldn't be dumb enough to get arrested for shooting a sheriff. But, we'll flush Logan out. We've got his woman. I wonder what he'll pay to get you back."

He untied her hands. "Get on your horse. You're coming with us."

Jen knew there was no way out. She wished she had concocted a better story. Something like Wolf had left her and she was no longer his woman. But, she doubted if Jesse would have believed her anyway. She was lucky he didn't talk to the operator, or he would know who had tipped them off. She knew since the jewels hadn't been on the stage, Barney had received her telegraph.

She was doubly glad that Jesse hadn't searched her thoroughly enough to find the receipt that she had stuffed in her camisole. She wished she could get rid of it before Jesse decided on a full body search. The thought made her skin crawl.

He helped Jen mount, and looked up at her. "Do I need to tie your hands?"

"I'll stay put. I'm more apt to fall off and slow you down if my hands are tied." Jen told him.

"It's a hassle to lead your horse. Come along peaceful and I'll let you ride by yourself. But try to run and Breed will drill you."

"Makes no never mind to me, you being a woman and all," Breed said.

"Let's go," Arizona said, kneeing his horse. Jen followed. She had no choice. Breed brought up the rear.

Chapter 17
Present

Jenny woke up shivering. She wanted to go back to sleep and find out what happened; in another way she was glad she was awake, and back in the present day.

She was beginning to wish the dreams would stop. They were getting scarier and scarier. What would happen if Jen was killed, would she die too? Or Wolf? If Wolf died, would Rand die?

That was what she worried about now. But, even if she didn't dream, would the inevitable happen anyway? Would she be better off knowing in advance, or was ignorance bliss?

The day was overcast and she had slept longer than she meant too. It was 6:45. Rand had said he would pick her up at 7. She had fifteen minutes to get home, or think up a real convincing excuse for not being home at 7 a.m.

It was a rush, but she turned into her driveway just as she saw Rand's pickup approaching from the other direction.

"You're out driving early this morning," Rand said, as he pulled up beside her Explorer and got out of his pickup. "You also don't look so good. You okay?"

All the excuses, "It's such a pretty morning; I wanted to take some photos,' 'I followed a stray cat,' flew out of

Jenny's head.

"I'm fine. I well, had a bad dream."

Rand's dark brows drew together. "You spent the night in Wild Rose again, didn't you?"

He looked so much like Wolf Jenny wondered if she was still dreaming. "You've been there at least three times. Why do you go there? It can't be that comfortable to sleep in this rig." He tapped the hood of the Explorer.

"I...I can't help it. The dreams, they, well, they pull at me. I get sick until I go to Wild Rose. I'm also... I'm afraid they will come here, and I'd rather keep them in Wild Rose then have them filter into my house."

"You're crazy. Don't you know how dangerous that can be. Don't open your mind to it. It's well, it could be demonic."

"I don't think they're demonic." Jenny had never thought about the dreams in those terms. Her family wasn't very religious.

"There's another whole world out there, and you can't dismiss all spiritual entities as either angels or demons. I don't think I'm in danger,"

Jenny put the thought of possibly dying if Jen died out of her mind. "And, I think I'm close to the end of the story. Last night Jen was kidnapped by Jesse Arizona. I don't know if Wolf is still alive, I don't know if he caught Sheriff Campbell, and I want to know the end of the story."

She talked very fast, and even to herself she knew the words sounded like scrambled garbage. Rand looked at her as if she had sprouted two heads, or turned into a bug-eyed gray alien.

"You must have a real active imagination," Rand said, shaking his head. "But, here in the present, we have a long drive. Are you ready?"

232

"Let me run inside a minute." Jen said. She wanted to quickly wash her face, dab on some make-up, and change into fresh clothes. She wished she could shower, but there was no time.

Ten minutes later she joined Rand, who was standing beside his pickup.

"Jump in," he said, opening driver's side door and letting Jenny scramble in. She sat beside him instead of scooting over into the passenger seat. Rand slid behind the wheel and shut the door.

"You can tell me the entire story on the way. Start with the first dream. So much going on, I kind of forgot all the details. Besides, I'm a sucker for a good ghost story."

Rand put the pickup into gear and backed out of Jenny's driveway.

Jenny took a deep breath, and recounted the entire story, starting with the very first dream.

Rand was a good listener, and when

she ran down, after recounting the episode where Jen was in Jesse Arizona's hands, Rand shook his head in amazement. "Wow! You should write western novels. That sounds like good story actually."

"One thing I have trouble with, though," Jenny said, "I see Wolf Logan, Barney Morgan and Jesse Arizona, they are all real characters." Jenny swept a stray piece of hair out of her eyes. "In fact, some of my research revealed that Barney Morgan helped to clean up corruption in Wild Rose, so the dreams seem to have a basis in fact. But, who is Jen? She must be real too, but where does she fit in?"

"We have an old trunk in the attic with letters and papers inside," Rand said thoughtfully. "Maybe photos too. We can go through that, and at least find the name of Great-Granddad Phelan's mom. I never thought about it, but I've never seen her name. Jen could be the missing name. I don't know if Wolf was married to her or not."

"You don't mind me prying into your family?" Jenny asked.

Rand shook his head. "No, I'm curious too. I'd like to find out more."

A car, driving wildly down the road, nearly sideswiped the pickup. Rand jerked the wheel to avoid a collision.

"Wow." Jenny's heart dropped from her throat back into her chest. "That was close. What a reckless driver."

"He is. I didn't get a real good look, but I thought it looked like Keith Miller. I didn't know he was back in this part of the country."

"You know him?"

Rand grunted. "Kind of."

He turned off the main road and followed a gravel road for several miles before steering off on a barely visible

two-track across a pasture. Topping a
hill, Jenny saw an open field that had a
green panel corral set up full of horses
and riders and young calves. The air
smelled of dust and horses and manure.

"What's a jackpot roping," Jenny
asked as Rand parked the pickup and got
out, holding out his hand to help Jenny
out of the pickup.

"Everyone's entry goes into a pot,"
Rand explained, still holding her hand as
they walked across the grass field
towards the arena. "Depending on how
many ropers enter, and how much the
entry fee is, the pot can be sizable. The
winner takes all, no second or third place.
I usually enter, but I can't swing a rope
today, I feel okay but the arm is still
stiff."

The roping was well attended, with
a lot of people sitting in the makeshift
seats, formed by laying planks across hay
bales. Others were sitting on tailgates of

pickups parked near the fence; some were sitting on the fence as well.

Rand lead Jenny to a plank seat, but he stood by the fence to get a closer look. After ducking her head to see the action through the green panels, Jenny gave up and went to stand beside Rand. He was talking to the cowboy next to him, who was kidding him about his accident, and wishing him a speedy recovery. Several others walked over to chat, and Jenny saw a gal waving at her from across the arena.

"Its Elsie," she told Rand, and Elsie left her group and came around the arena to see them.

"Hey, Jenny. Rand, thought you might be here. Good to see you out and about. How's the shoulder? Good crowd here today, I hear the jackpot is around $700. Good money."

"Hi, Elsie," Rand was used to Elsie's rapid fire questions. "Shoulder's fine, healing well, good crowd, and, yeah, it's a pretty good pot. Wish I was in the running for it."

He fell silent as another calf was turned loose the rider spurred his big, colorful Appaloosa horse in pursuit.

"That's a lot of money for one afternoon," Jenny said to Elsie, as Rand was intent on the roper, who quickly caught the calf and leaped off his horse to throw it down and tie it.

"Not bad," Elsie said.   "Dean's pretty good, he wins a lot." she nodded towards the roper, who had thrown up his hands to indicate that he had completed his tie. "He made good time," Elsie said. "The fastest go so far."

Action was fast. Roper after roper left the chute, roped and tied the calf, or missed and had to take a 'no time.' The number of contestants dwindled, with Dean and his colorful black and white spotted horse catching and tying calf after calf.   Rand cheered him on, yelling insulting but friendly comments.

"Did they grow up together?" Jenny asked Elsie, after Dean won the jackpot and Rand left to congratulate him on his win.

Elsie grinned.   "Yeah, and they were always in trouble too. What one didn't think up, the other did. Gramps used to call them Jesse and Cole, after Jesse James and Cole Younger."

Jenny smiled. "Who was who?"

"Rand was Jesse, of course. He was usually the ring leader."

Elsie nodded towards the action in the arena. "Him and Dean usually go back and forth on winning these, sometimes Rand wins, sometimes Dean does. I don't think they purposely take turns, but who knows. It's all in good fun, though. Today, I heard that Dean owes Rand money, so Rand wanted to get him to 'pay up' while he's still got his winnings."

Jenny giggled, "So that's why Rand was cheering for him so enthusiastically. Not friendship, just filthy lucre."

Elsie laughed, and they dissolved into a fit of giggles, made worse by Rand coming back and asking them what the joke was. They refused to tell him, and, shaking his head at the quirkiness of women, he turned to Dean and asked about an upcoming roping, walking with Dean to his pickup and horse trailer and leaving the girls to follow.

After Dean loaded his horse, Rand turned to Jenny.

"I think a beer is in order," he said. "How about it Dean, Elsie? Want to go to the Ranger?"

"If you're buying," Dean grinned.

"Sure," Elsie said.

Rand and Jenny lead the parade back to Crystal Creek, and the only bar in town. Dean and Elsie followed close behind.

Even though the roping had been held several miles away, the bar was crowded with ropers. Rand found a table and pulled out a chair for Jenny, a touch of chivalry Jenny found enjoyable. Elsie seated herself, and Rand asked, "What do you gals want to drink? I'll go get it, probably quicker than waiting for the waitress."

Looking at the nearly shoulder to shoulder cowboys, Jenny had to agree. She was surprised that they actually found a table, but many of the men were sitting or standing near the bar.

"I'll have a Negra," Elsie said. "With lots of lime."

Beer seemed to be the order of the day. "Negra's fine with me," Jenny said. "I'll take some limes too."

"Right back," Rand said, and Dean, having to park further away with the stock trailer, came through the door, and caught Rand's eye before coming over to the table with the girls.

"If Rand's playing waiter, I'll stay here." Dean smiled, taking off his hat and setting it carefully, crown up, on the table.

"Great roping today," Elsie said. "This is Jenny Morgan , she's new in town."

"Nice to meet you," Dean said, reaching a long arm across the table to shake Jenny's hand.

"Same," Jenny said.   Dean was good looking, with sandy brown hair and sky-blue eyes that danced engagingly, but Jenny had the feeling he looked that way at every girl.

Suddenly, the chatter from the bar seemed to stop.   Silence fell over the room.

"Wow," Dean said, looking at the bar. The drinkers split into two factions, and Rand, carefully setting the drinks back on the bar, faced the other man. He was about Rand's age, with slicked back blond hair and a shark-like face.

"I know that bitch Linda is here somewhere, probably crying on your shoulder, Logan," he said.

"Trouble," Elsie whispered to Jenny. "Linda and Rand were engaged, but she went out on him and married Keith Miller. He's a wife beater and an all around mean SOB. Linda left him, I hope it's for good this time."

"I haven't seen Linda in three years," Rand said. He was standing easy with his back to the bar, obviously not worried. "Go home and sober up, Miller." He started to turn away, but Miller grabbed his arm.

"Don't turn your back on me, g..damn it," Miller said, pulling at Rand's arm.

Rand turned so quick that Jenny was surprised. He spun around, and landed a left hook on Miller's jaw that sent him staggering backward into his friends, who pushed him upright and back towards Rand.

"Rand's got a hurt shoulder," Jenny gasped.

"Take it outside," the bartender said.

Wiping the blood off his lip, Keith looked as if he would like to argue the fact, but his friends surrounded him and the crowd moved towards the door.

Jenny and Elsie looked at each other, then rose and followed the crowd outside.

Surprisingly, when they got outside, Rand was standing on the sidelines; surreptitiously nursing his shoulder and watching as Dean and Keith slugged it out, but it was easy to see that Keith was out classed.

"Dean's a black belt in Judo and Taekwondo," Elsie said. "He loves martial arts, weird, isn't it. Rand's good too, but Dean's better. He wins a lot at the Friday night fights in Red Bluffs."

It didn't take long. Dean met Keith's first awkward rush, blocking Kieth's punch and countering with a right to Keith's stomach, followed with a hard left to his jaw. Keith was out for the count.

Dean wasn't even breathing hard, but he was rubbing the knuckles on his left hand.

Keith's friends were bending over him, slapping his face.

"Does he need an ambulance," one guy asked.

"He's fine," Dean said. "Just take him home and he can sleep it off."

Keith groaned and, with help, set up, groggily shaking his head.

His friends helped him up and escorted him into a pickup.

Jenny wanted to ask Rand if he was

okay, and what happened that Dean ended the fight, but she wasn't sure if she should say anything. She and Elsie trailed along behind the guys, and returned to the table. Dean went up to the bar, picked up the untouched drinks and brought them back to the table and sat down.

"How did that happen?" Elsie asked.

Rand laughed. "We sort of accused Keith of being a coward and picking on a cripple. He felt bulletproof, and boasted he could take on both of us. Dean agreed to go first. Thanks, buddy." Rand said, acknowledging Dean's help, and taking a long swallow of his Budweiser.

Rand glanced at Jenny, and half raised his beer in salute to her, and grinned at her. She smiled back, sipping on her beer.

Ropers crowded around their table, replaying the fight, giving Dean good-natured ribbing.

"Hell, Miller never could fight worth a damn, unless he's beating on someone smaller and weaker," He said.

"Like Linda," Elsie said under her breath.

"Really?" Jenny asked softly.

"Yeah. Linda went to the Women's Shelter, and now no one really knows where she is. She has a restraining order against Miller."

Jenny looked at her. "You know where she is?"

"Let's go outside," Elsie said, standing up.

Jenny stood up and followed Elsie, sensing that Elsie wanted to talk. She followed Elsie to a small, grassy area outside the bar.

"I volunteer once a week at the Women's Shelter." Elsie said, in answer to Jenny's question. "Ever since Mom and I had to run away from that jerk she married. My father died when I was ten, and Mom married this jerk Mike. Was with him about two years. He started drinking and began to beat on Mom and me. One day I ran to Gramps, told him was was happening, and Gramps came in the next day with a shotgun, told Mom to get packed, he was taking us to his ranch. Then he told Mike if he ever saw him again Gramps would shoot him. Mike believed him. Mom died of cancer three years ago, and I've been taking care of Gramps ever since. That's why I volunteer there. I want to help other women in those situations."

"Good for you." Jenny said, wishing she could do something as useful. Maybe she could. "I wish I lived here full time, I'd volunteer myself. Maybe I can in Billings.

"I'm sure you could. I didn't mean to dump on you, but sometimes I feel the need to talk about it, especially when something like the Miller thing brings it all to the surface again. Thanks for listening." She smiled at Jenny, and Jenny smiled back, feeling a sudden connection to Elsie she hadn't felt before.

When they returned to the table, the guys finished their beers, and Dean said he had to get his rope horse home. "Think the old boy pulled a muscle in his shoulder," Dean said, shrugging his own shoulders, "and I might have pulled something too. But it was worth it to put that jackass on the ground."

"I was great to watch," Rand commented as they walked to the pickups.

"Well," Rand said, glancing at his watch. "I can't do much around the ranch yet, but it gives me an excuse to take a little time off. What if I drop you off at your house, go home and change into a better shirt, and take you out to supper and a movie." He started the pickup and pulled away from the bar.

Jenny felt he social life was taking a big leap forward, and with Rand! There was no hesitation in her reply, and her smile was wide. "I'd love to. What time will you be back?" They were at her house now, and she was preparing to open the door and jump out.

"About 5?"

"Sounds good, I'll be ready," she said.

On the drive to Red Bluffs, Rand and Jenny visited, learning more about each other. He took her to supper at *Ranchers*, a nice restaurant that served beef and seafood. Rand had a porterhouse, and Jenny ordered steak and wood grilled shrimp. Over supper Rand told her how much Red Bluffs had changed over the years, saying that when he was growing up it was almost totally agriculture, with the many ranchers growing wheat in addition to cattle, and in the irrigated valley, sugar beets.

"Now, most of the irrigated land is in hay, and a big part of the economy is tourism. Which is okay I guess," Rand said, cutting his steak and commenting, "One upside is that there are better restaurants in town."

"Always a plus," Jenny laughed. Her meal was excellent, and she didn't feel any pull tonight to visit the ghost town. Maybe being with Rand stilled the ghosts. She would have liked to find out what happened to Jen, but she wanted to spend time with Rand even more.

She told him about growing up in Bismark, ND and then moving to Billings when she was in high school. "My life isn't all that exciting," she said. "I'm having fun, sort of, with this writing project, and I like this area. I didn't know I was such a small town girl until I came here."

When they finished and Rand paid

the bill he asked her which movie she wanted to see. "There's one with Bill Murray, or a western. We've only got two choices."

Thinking of Wolf Logan, Jenny chose the western, and it turned out to be a good choice. Rand held her hand during the movie, and at one point put his arm around her shoulders. She was glad she sat on his left, his right shoulder was probably still sore.

"That was a good movie," Rand said as they left the theater two hours later. It was still light in the west, but darkness was crouching on the horizon.

Rand drove home slowly, and Jenny wondered if he planned to park along the way, and how she would handle it if he was looking for a roll in the hay, so to speak.

Nothing happened. Rand kept the pickup at a steady speed, slowing down only once for a nervous deer that ran across the road, slipping and sliding on the pavement. Her fawn, almost invisible in the tall grass, dived out after her, but Rand, expecting that, hadn't got back to road speed and let them both cross the highway safely.

When they got to Jenny's house, Rand walked her to her door and waited while Jenny unlocked the it, then took her in his arms.

Being careful of his shoulder, Jenny returned the kiss, and felt the hard muscles of Rand's chest against her breasts. She could taste the shot of Baileys Irish Cream that Rand had sipped as an after dinner drink, and she could smell his Old Spice aftershave.

"Thanks for the wonderful day and night," Jenny told him. "I really enjoyed it."

"I did too," Rand said, smiling at her. She watched his lean body as he jumped into the pickup, and watched the

Silverado until it was out of sight around a curve.

She hugged herself, reliving the movie and the goodnight kiss. She had to tell herself it was probably just a summer fling, but deep down she hoped for more. Much more.

She turned and went into her house.

Chapter 18
Present

Jenny expected the pull as soon as she walked into the dark house. Nothing came. She had to grope for the light switch, finally found it and the light pushed the darkness away. Maybe she no longer needed to go to the ghost town, but she wondered what happened to Jen, and to Wolf. Maybe she'd never find out. Possibly the time had something to do with it. Maybe it was like midnight, and once the dreaming hour had passed, the call no longer came.

Tonight, after a day in the open air and later the movie, she didn't care a whole lot. She was tired and the bed looked inviting, after the nights spent in the car. She tumbled into bed, and didn't wake until the early morning sun tickled her eyelids. The ringing of the phone might have had something to do with it as well.

"Jenny? Rand. How are you this morning?"

"Fine. It looks like a beautiful day out there. How are you?"

"Good, good. Say, Mom said you might like to go riding sometime and we have to move some heifers today. I'm going to ride, but I don't feel like working too hard, so we could use an extra hand. Want to go?"

"I'd like that," Jenny said, suppressing the urge to comment that Rand, only out of the hospital a few days, shouldn't be riding. He had one mother. If he felt well enough to ride, it wasn't any of her business. "What time."

"We're getting the horses in right now. Just come on out."

On the drive to the Logan ranch Jenny had time to think again about her dreams, and why last night had been barren.

Had the dreams ended as suddenly as they came? Would she ever find out what happened to Wolf and Jen in the hands of Jesse Arizona? Jenny had done enough research already on Barney Morgan's life to know that, many times, the entire story would never be known.

If Wolf and Jen had been killed, she may never know. Even old newspapers might not allude to the fact that a bounty hunter and his mistress met with a sad end. But, she felt like there was more to the story. She wanted to find out what happened, but she wasn't sure how.

She would go to Wild Rose again tonight. But, for now, she had to put the past out of her mind, and concentrate on Rand Logan. Somehow, that wouldn't be too hard to do.

She was a little surprised to see that at the Logan ranch, moving cattle was a family affair. Betty, Rand and Waylyn were all at the corral. She was glad that Betty was going. She still wasn't totally comfortable with Rand's family, and having another woman along would be nice.

Rand came out of the large barn, leading a small, neatly built brown and white pinto, that he gravely introduced to Jenny. "Jenny, this is Kid," she almost expected him to say, "Kid, meet Jenny."

"Kid is gentle, but he knows his business, which is cows. If a cow starts to turn back, Kid will go after it, and he can turn mighty quick," he grinned. "There's no shame if you have to grab ahold of the saddle horn."

"Have you ridden much Jenny?" Betty asked.

"Not for a long time. I had a friend in high school who had horses and we used to ride some. I would have liked a horse like this when I was a horse-crazy kid." She stroked Kid's long, bony face.

Rand held Kid while Jenny mounted, and then he adjusted the stirrups to the length of her legs. Finishing, he slapped her gently on the leg. "Ready, cowhand?"

Jenny grinned, remembering the line in the movie, *'Smokey and the Bandit,'* 'I was born ready,' but she smiled and just said, "Ready."

She enjoyed feeling the horse move under her, and seeing the grasslands that made up the Logan ranch. For some reason, the insides of her thighs and her knees, where they touched the stirrup leathers, felt sore, as if she had been riding recently.   Just in her dream, she remembered.

Rand rode beside her, and the heifers trotted along in front of the riders, sensing they were moving to better pastures.   Their calves trotted along beside the mother-cows, occasionally bouncing off the path to investigate a bush or a tall weed. They were cute little critters, in almost every color known to cattle. Jenny laughed at their antics as they ran and jumped like colorful jackrabbits.

"They seem like well-trained cows," she commented to Rand, thinking of TV westerns, where the cows were running every direction, and the cowboys galloped and waved ropes and yelled.

"Some ranchers handle the cows pretty rough, and they get kind of spooky. We like to work ours slow and easy, less stress on them and us. During the winter we can move them back and forth from pasture to pasture with a pickup and a bucket of cow cake."

"Chocolate or white?" Jenny asked, smiling.

"Corn." Rand grinned, "Plus, they go this way every summer about this time."

He left her side momentarily when a heifer left the road for an irresistible bite of grass. The heifer saw Rand's black horse bear down on her but she grabbed a mouthful of grass before returning to the trail.

They put the heifers through a gate with tall poles and a wire twisted between them across the top, turned the horses back to towards the house, Waylyn and Betty leading them on a different trail that Rand told her was a short cut back to the house, and they could check a water tank on the way as well.

They were about half way back, by Jenny's reckoning, when Rand pointed to a depression in the ground with a few blackened timbers and a some jumbled rocks.

"Wolf Logan's homestead, or what's left of it anyway," he told Jenny.

The ground shimmered. The grasses waved gently, then more violently. The cabin ruins were no longer ruins, but they were a cabin, a cabin which suddenly burst into flames.

A man galloped up on a black horse. He jerked the horse to a stop, leaped off and ran towards the flames. It was Wolf. Even if Jenny hadn't recognized the horse, she would have recognized his tall form, and the easy movement of his body. Before the vision faded, she could have sworn that she heard a plaintive child voice crying, "Daddy, Daddy, over here." Then, the ruins were ruins again, and Kid was dancing under her and Rand was looking at her strangely.

"What happened, are you sick?" Rand asked.

"I don't know," Jenny said. "I feel a little dizzy, I think I'd better sit down for a minute."

She started to dismount, and Rand was there. He helped her down off the horse, and led her over to a patch of grass that was free of cactus and sagebrush so she could sit.

Jenny pulled her knees up, put her head down on them, waiting until the dizzy feeling passed. She felt like a fool in front of Rand's family, but she couldn't help it.

Betty had dismounted, and came over beside them. She touched Jenny on the shoulder. "Are you sure you're okay? Maybe it's the heat."

Jenny raised her head "I think I'm okay now,"

"You look pretty white, can you ride? Maybe we should come back with the pickup and trailer," Betty said to Rand.

"We'll just wait a minute," Rand said. "You and Dad go ahead, if we're not back in 45 minutes, come out with the horse trailer."

"That's a good idea," Waylyn said. He had dismounted as well, but was getting ready to remount. "We can bring the trailer, Jenny, it might be better."

Betty got back on her tall bay, and Rand watched them ride away.

"Now, what happened? You felt something there, didn't you?"

Rand knew about the dreams, so it didn't bother Jenny to tell him. In fact, she was sure that was why Rand sent his family on ahead, so she could tell him without an audience.

"I saw Wolf's cabin. I saw it go up in flames. I saw Wolf and I heard a child's voice calling "Daddy, Daddy,"

"Hum." Rand said, taking a long

264

piece of grass and chewing on it thoughtfully. Kid nudged Jenny with his nose, and Jenny stroked it absently.

She had a feeling that Rand wanted to tell her something, but then he changed his mind. "Feel better now?" he asked.

"Yeah, I think I'm okay now."

Rand helped her mount Kid, and they rode side by side until the trail narrowed going up a hill and Kid fell behind Raven.

"What do you think causes those visions?" Rand asked after they topped the hill.

Jenny nudged Kid up alongside Raven, who reached over to nip at Kid. Rand jigged him with his spur and Raver subsided with bad grace. Jenny laughed at the horses' by-play.

"I don't know. I've been wondering that. Is something from the past going to affect my future? I'm not sure," Jenny said. She wondered about the newest vision, a vision in broad daylight was unusual, and she wondered if it would be repeated. It was getting really scary.

"Did Wolf's cabin burn down?" Jenny asked.

Rand shrugged. "I guess so, due to the fact that the timbers at the ruins are charred. I'll have to ask Pa. I'm not exactly sure what happened." Jenny had a feeling that he wasn't telling the entire truth, but she didn't press him.

"Still feeling okay?" He asked, changing the subject.

"I'm fine now. It was just the vision I guess. I've never had one in the daylight before."

"Think you'll feel good enough to go to a street dance with me tonight? It's the annual Crystal Creek Days kickoff. Lots of activities."

"Sure," Jenny said. "Sounds like fun." Another date. Things were really looking up in the romance department. "What time?"

"About 8." Rand said. On the rest of the ride home he was full of stories about the ranch, and the people who homesteaded in the area in the early part of the century. He didn't refer to Wolf or his homestead again, and Jenny wondered if he were talking about everything else to keep her from questioning him on the subject. She was enjoying the ride, and didn't want to talk about anything that might kill Rand's light-hearted mood.

Back at Rand's house, she helped him un-saddle the horses and turn them out to pasture.

"Glass of iced tea for the road?" Rand asked, and Jenny gratefully accepted the offer.

She wondered if Rand would remember what he had said about some old trunk in the attic, but before she

could ask Waylyn said something about
fixing a tractor, and Rand said, "See you
tonight," before following his father out.

When she got back to her house she
took a long, hot bath to soak away some
of the soreness from the ride, and entered
the newest vision into her computer.
Then, thinking of what might be a late
night, she lay down for a nap and didn't
wake until the alarm clock went off at
five.

She dressed in a long denim skirt
and a lacy blouse. She had picked them
up on her last trip to Billings, hoping that
she would find a place to wear them.
Now was a good time.

She was glad when she saw the
admiration in Rand's face. She could
hear the band tuning up as they left her
house.

Most of the residents of Crystal
Creek and the surrounding communities
were in evidence at the dance. The street

was blocked off with ropes and hay bales, giving a rustic look to the dance, but the band, a local group which had a good enough sound, was elevated on a flat bed trailer. "I think a hay wagon would have been more appropriate," Jenny whispered to Rand.

He grinned and whispered back. "I know the drummer. I'll mention it to him for next time."

The dance area was full of people; youngsters, married couples, and even an older man who belied his advanced years by his performance of an active jitterbug with an attractive older lady wearing a colorful square-dancer skirt.

"Your folks here?" she asked Rand.

Rand shook his head. "Pa don't dance, and Mom gave up trying to convince him too. They enjoy staying home in the evenings anyway."

"Hey, Rand, Jenny," Elsie was sitting on a hay bale next to Dean. "Good time, huh, look at Gramps." she nodded towards the older gent that Jenny had seen cutting up the makeshift dance floor. "He can still cut quite a figure, no?"

"He sure do," Rand grinned. "He never misses a dance, does he?"

The band ended the song, and the next one was a slower song, *Amarillo by Morning*, which they did fairly well. It was one of Jenny's favorites, and she was glad when Rand lead her out on the street and took her in his arms.

It seemed so right, her body molded against his, her head on this shoulder, and the soft country music. She could smell the scent of his Old Spice cologne, and his brush popper shirt was soft against her cheek. They stayed on the floor through that song, and the next one, *Blue Eyes Crying in the Rain*. The stars came out, and the street lights cast a soft glow on the scene. Jenny forgot everything except being in Rand's arms, swaying to the music.

It was so perfect that Jenny didn't realize for a moment that the scene was subtlety shifting. The dancers were no longer wearing Wrangler shirts and jeans, but buckskins and homespun. The women weren't in jeans and modern dresses, but in long, full skirts. The music changed from modern country to the old classic song, *In the Sweet, Bye and Bye*. And, she wasn't dancing with Rand, she was dancing with Wolf.

Jenny blinked her eyes, trying to clear her senses. The present came back, and Rand was whispering in her ear, "Are you okay?"

It was Rand holding her, not Wolf. The singer was singing *Kentucky Rain*, an old Elvis song. It was a reminder that she was in the modern world, not in the past. "In the cold Kentucky Rain," the singer crooned.

"I'm fine. I guess I'm still a little off

kilter like I was this morning. Can we sit out the next song? And could we find a Coke or something?"

"Coke or something stronger, but maybe a Coke is better," Rand said, and his breath stirred the hair and tickled her ear.

They sat side by side on a straw bale, and Jenny sipped the Coke Rand found for her in a cooler. Dean and Elsie joined them.

"How's the shoulder, Rand?" Dean asked.

"Getting better. I rode today, no problems." Rand took a swallow of his beer. "Have you seen anything more of Bill?"

"Naw, he's like a big rat that scuttles away when the dog starts digging. I doubt that he'll show his face again."

"Like Mike," Elsie said.

Again, Jenny felt a great respect for

Henry. And for Dean. She also felt a great respect for Elsie. To have gone through that and came through it was something that Jenny couldn't even imagine.

A large, muscular lady, who wouldn't have looked out of place on a Harley, Jenny thought, swayed over with a tray full of beers. "Blackie bought these for you," she said, handing everyone a beer.

Jenny was rather surprised to see that the woman handed her and Elsie each a Negra Modelo. Small towns again. The waitress remembered what they drank. Of course, Elsie had been here often. Everyone knew her.

"Thanks," Rand said. "Put one my tab for him."

"Will do. How's the shoulder, you gonna be in the country rodeo?"

"If not, it's better for me," Dean said. "I'll be assured of the first place buckle then. Maybe I should slap his shoulder a few times to keep him crippled."

"You do and I'll slug you," Rand said with a grin.

"On second thought, I'll just have a dance with your lady. Care for a dance, Jenny?"

Not sure what protocol was in Wyoming, Jenny glanced at Rand, who grinned and motioned with his beer towards the dance floor.

She rose and followed Dean. He was a good dancer, but not as good as Rand, or was she a little prejudice? They danced a slow dance, then stayed on the floor or a jitterbug.

Rand and Elsie were on the floor, and Jenny wondered about them, they seemed so at ease with each other, she wondered if they had once been a couple, and she felt a stab of jealousy.

Dean was an exuberant dancer, and

after the jitterbug Jenny laughed and declared she was thirsty, again, and they returned to the hay bale, and Rand and Elsie joined them.

They taught Jenny to line dance, and then she joined them in the butterfly polka, first she and Elsie partnered Rand, and then Jenny and Rand shared it with Dean, while Elsie and her grandpa partnered with Laura, the lady Henry had been dancing with earlier.

After the dance a tall, gray-haired man sauntered over to speak to Rand and was introduced to Jenny.

"Jenny Morgan, Blackie Hart." Rand said, and Blackie nodded to her before talking to Rand briefly.

After he left to talk to another rancher, Rand told Jenny, "Blackie is a retired deputy from the county sheriff's office. Everyone behaves better when he's around. He can't officially arrest anyone, but if Blackie was to call the cop shop, they'd listen and be down here immediately. He could handle about anything until they got here."

Rand took a drink of his beer.

"He heard something about the fight with Miller, and advised me to watch out for him. I assured him I would."

Jenny felt better just knowing that Blackie was around, and she felt nothing really bad would happen if he were there.

The dance ended at one a.m. The last dance was a slow dance to George Strait's, *I Cross My Heart*. Rand held Jenny close as they danced. It felt so right, and Jenny hoped that it could go on this way for, well, she wasn't quite willing to say forever, but she hoped it would last a long time. She had never felt so much a part of any group since high school.

Rand helped with some of the cleaning up, then drove Jenny home. When they stopped in front of Jenny's house, he leaned across the seat and reached for her. She moved into his arms, and felt the tingles run up her body as his lips explored her neck, and then moved across her cheek to capture her lips.

She parted her lips, and felt his tongue explore the soft reaches of her mouth, and she explored his, loving the feelings he aroused in her. She stroked his neck, and tangled her fingers in his dark hair.

His hand moved across her chest, unbuttoning her shirt to work his fingers under her lacy bra to feel the soft skin beneath.

Suddenly, the scent of Rand's spicy aftershave was replace by the smell of buckskin and campfire smoke. She tensed, and moved back slightly, opening her eyes to look at Rand.

It wasn't Rand, it was Wolf. Confused, she pulled away. The features were again Rand's, but the mood was broken.

"It's late," he said, moving her gently away from him, buttoning up her shirt. "I've got to go."

"Rand?"

He leaned over and kissed her again.   "There's someone else there, behind your eyes. When he's gone, I'll be glad to continue.   Who is he, someone back in Billings?"

She wished he wasn't so nice. He had the right to be angry if he felt she was stringing him along, using him to make someone else jealous, or, even worse, using Rand for a summer fling, which would end when she returned to her life in Billings.

"No, really, there's no one else, no one in Billings, I...I can't explain it, but there's no one else, I'm not stringing you along, honest."

"Whatever you say. But I do have to get home. Early riser, ya' know. Good night, Jenny."

Jenny watched the taillights of Rand's pickup until they disappeared around a bend in the road. She hoped he hadn't driven out of her life for good. She regretted the way the evening ended, and cursed Wolf Logan for interfering.

"He's your great-great-grandson, so don't interfere," She told the universe at large and hoped that Wolf heard her, if the dead could communicate with the living.

Maybe they could. Even though it was nearly 3 am. and would be daylight soon, Jenny jumped into her car and headed down the familiar blacktop to Wild Rose. The dreams had to come again. She had to find out the rest of the story, and maybe tell Wolf Logan to butt out of her life.

Chapter 19
1885

Jen was sitting in a small, rough, boarded room, her hands tied tightly behind her. The rope rubbed her wrists but she kept twisting her hands anyway, trying to loosen the knots.

A single coal oil lamp provided little light, just a circle around the table top where Arizona and the man called Breed and a woman sat talking. A whiskey bottle was sitting in front of

Jesse, and occasionally he would raise the bottle, take a long swallow, and hand it over to 'Breed.

Jen wondered who the woman was. She was pretty, in a harsh sort of way, with brassy blond hair pulled back in a long braid.

"Can you deliver the message?" Jesse asked the woman.

The woman gave a harsh, sardonic laugh. "It will be a pleasure. I can't wait to see the look on Wolf's face when he sees me. It will be like seeing a ghost." She laughed again. "He thinks I'm dead."

"Damn it, Molly. I told you who to give the message to, that little red-headed whore at Miss Lou's, and she'll make sure he gets it. You don't walk up to Wolf Logan and say, 'Arizona has your woman.' He'd probably shoot you dead. He'll get here, and he'll see you soon enough."

"Are you sure he'll come. Maybe he doesn't care enough for his whore."

Jen twisted against the ropes again, but they were still tight. She felt a nail break to the quick but pain was nothing compared to her indignation. A whore was she? No way. If she could get free, she would find a way to shoot them all. But first she would like the satisfaction of clawing the woman's arrogant face.

Arizona grinned wolfishly. "He'll come. Even if he doesn't care about her, he has his pride. He'll discover I took one woman from him, and he'll be damned if I'll take another. Even if you came willingly, and she didn't, it don't matter."

The woman leaned over and kissed Arizona on the cheek. "Yeah, I wasn't abducted," she laughed. Jesse pulled her head down and kissed her full lips, then turned back to studying a map laid out on the table.

Then the woman came over to Jen, bending over her. Jen could smell the woman's sweet, heavy perfume, and she saw the turquoise earrings that swung from the woman's ears. With a shock, Jen recognized the earrings as a match to the necklace that Wolf had given her. The tiny carved wolves were miniature versions on the one on her necklace.

"He'll come for you, won't he honey? At least you want to believe that. Wouldn't you?" Molly said, running a finger down Jen's cheek.

Jen didn't answer her question. "Your earrings," she said.

Molly touched one gently. "I used to have a necklace that matched them. I lost it somewhere."

Jen felt a shiver run up her spine, and hoped that the woman and Jesse didn't unbutton her shirt and discover the necklace on her neck. Molly might claim prior ownership and take it back.

But even more stunning was the implication. This woman was the one

Wolf was mumbling about when he was wounded. The one he thought Arizona had killed. But he hadn't killed her. She had run off with Arizona, leaving Wolf and his boy. That was worse than if she had been killed or abducted. She had left Wolf of her own free will, ran off with his enemy. Jen tried to let her contempt show in her eyes as she looked at Molly.

Maybe it had, because Molly gave her an odd look and went back to the table with Arizona and Breed. "We should have stuck to rustling," Breed was saying. "There's more money in that then in woman stealing."

"This one could be worth quite a bit," Jesse said. "I know what I'm doing, Breed. Logan will come for her, and we'll get Logan. Then, we can go back to lifting those payrolls and gold shipments."

But the other man wasn't satisfied. "Look, Jesse," He said, jerking his head towards Jen. "She telegraphed for the Marshall or someone. I don't believe her story about telling the sheriff. I think your hatred for Logan is over riding your good sense."

Arizona's face turned an ugly red. "Look, Breed, if you don't like the way I'm running this, you can leave. Once Wolf's out of the way, there's no proof of anything. Campbell can 'arrest' us and we can escape again, and lay low until the marshals and the judges get tired of waiting."

"I still say you should make this whore talk. You don't know if she did send a message, and you don't know how much Logan knows."

Jesse rubbed his chin. "For once, you may be right."

He came over and knelt beside Jen, taking her chin in his hand and turning her face toward him. His breath smelled of whiskey and stale tobacco. She tried to turn her head away.

"Wolf still has good taste in women," He laughed, running a calloused finger across Jen's cheek. She jerked away from his touch, and he laughed.

"Feisty, too. That's another thing we think alike on," He grinned up at Molly. "But she's not like you, is she. I'll bet she's not as hard edged." Molly gave him a chilly smile, and turned away, obviously not liking the attention he was giving Jen. Jen knew she might be able to use that to her advantage.

He laughed and twirled a strand of Jen's hair around his finger, looking at Molly. He tugged at it hard enough to hurt. "Now, missy what did you put in the telegraph, and who did you send it too."

"I told you, I didn't send it. If I had, all it said was, "have necessary information."

"And who was this to be sent too?"

Breed drew a long-bladed knife and spat on his whet stone, running the blade across it gently. The sound of it rasping on the stone set Jen's teeth on edge. But she remained silent, staring at Jesse with contempt.

Jesse grunted. "Who did you send it to?"

Jen remained silent.

Arizona's hand drew back and shot out, the force of the slap making Jen's head jerk back, and she felt an explosion of pain in cheek bone.

"I can get it out of her," Breed said, running his thumb down the knife blade. The blade caught the light and gleamed.

"Now, tell me who you sent that telegram too, or I'll turn Breed here lose with his knife. A pretty picture you'd make when Logan finds you, all carved up like a butchered heifer."

Jen discarded several possible lies,

and decided that it wasn't worth getting dead for, besides, the telegram had sent, and nothing could change that. Barney Morgan was probably already in Wild Rose anyway, and if they had Campbell, he probably squealed anyway.   He seemed like the type.

"Okay, I sent it to Judge Barney Morgan. In Rocky Point."

"Hell!" Jesse said. He left Jen and walked back to the table. "Even Morgan can't act with Wolf's testimony," Breed said. "As long as Wolf's dead, we don't need to worry." He re-sheathed his knife.

Suddenly, Breed threw up his hands and fell forward over the table. A crash of gunfire sounded almost simultaneously. Jen saw a neat hole in the grease-paper cover of the window.

Jesse dived to the floor just as another shot rang out. The next bullet shattered the chimney of the lamp, dousing the feeble flame. Now the only light was from the full moon, which was trying to struggle in through the grease-paper windows.

Arizona rolled over to Jen and grabbed her by the shoulder, jerking her to her feet as he stood up.

Molly crawled over to them, and Jesse handed her the revolver.

"Logan, I know it's you. I've got your woman here, and any shot may kill her. Come on in if you want her dead."

There was silence outside, and no more shots. The ropes on Jenny's arms were chaffing painfully, and she wondered what would happen next.

Wolf's harsh voice broke the stillness. "I have Campbell. I'd be willing to make a trade."

"We don't need Campbell. Kill the double crosser." Jesse yelled back.

"Sit down," Jesse hissed in Jen's ear. "And keep quiet. Molly can you cover the window?"

"What about the woman?"

"She's tied. Watch the window."

Jen worked frantically on the knots, but they had tied her tight. Next to her on the floor she saw a piece of the broken lamp chimney. She scooted around and her fingers found a sharp piece of the glass. She used it to saw at the ropes, and she felt one give. But she needed to cut through more to get free. Breed's body had fallen a few feet from her, and if she could get his knife....

Slowly, so as not to draw attention to herself, she wiggled across the floor, and, ignoring her revulsion to his dead body, she found the hilt of the knife. It took some doing, but she slipped it out of the scabbard, and began sawing on the remaining ropes, feeling them give as the sharp blade cut the strands. Suddenly, she was free. The ropes fell away. Picking up the knife, she hid it in the waist band of her jeans, and waited.

Breed's gun. She wondered if she could get it without them seeing her move.

"He's out there somewhere," Jesse said softly to Molly.

The only sound in the room was the jerky breathing of Jesse and Molly. Then, the silence was broken by the sound of gravel sliding off the tin roof. Jesse fired upward, the heavy bullet tearing a hole in the cabin roof.

Jenny took advantage of the confusion to scramble up and make a dive for the gun on Breed's hip. She had almost pulled it from the holster when Molly's booted foot came down on her hand, crushing it to the floor.

Jen let go of the gun and grabbed Molly's ankle, jerking Molly off balance. There was no time now to get Breed's gun, she had to concentrate on not being shot by Molly.

Molly had fallen against the table, but quickly regained her balance, and was concentrating on cocking the hammer of the revolver back, training it on Jen. Jen rolled over and rolled into Molly's legs, knocking her down and sending the gun skittering across the floor. Jen and Molly both crawled across the floor towards the gun. Jen got there first, and she felt the gun settle into her hand, then the cabin door burst open and a gun roared.

Molly grabbed for gun the gun in Jen's hand. With surprising strength she twisted it from Jen's still numbed fingers and swung it towards the familiar silhouette in the moonlit doorway. Desperately, Jen rolled her body into Molly's trying to throw off her aim.

Daylight poured in, the 20th century returned.

Chapter 20
Present

Jenny desperately wanted to go back to sleep, to find out what happened. Did Wolf get killed, or did Jen's frantic lunge knock off Molly's aim? But, she was worried about Rand as well. If Wolf had been killed, was Rand alright?

Jenny's wrists were raw and sore. She some aloe gel back at the house. That should help. She knew she couldn't get back to sleep, even if the dreams would come in the daylight. Still, it was with reluctance that she left the ghost town.

Back at her house, she smoothed aloe lotion on her wrists and felt the cooling salve relieve the soreness.

She was worried about Rand. She remembered his shoulder wound, just like Wolf's. Her own wrists, rubbed raw as if by harsh ropes. Even if she came across as a pushy, neurotic female, she had to find out. She could thank him again for the fun evening.

She dialed the Logan number, but no one answered. Logically, she knew they were probably outside working, but she was working herself in a state of high anxiety. She had to find out.

Jumping into her SUV, she headed to the Logan ranch, driving faster than she normally would have on the gravel road.

When she drove under the Logan

Longhorns sign, she saw Rand saddling up Raven. To her immense relief, he looked fine. In fact, he looked great. She parked her car near the corral and got out.

"Must be ESP," Rand grinned. "I though about inviting you to go riding again, I have to go out and check a back-country reservoir, but I thought you might be sleeping in. Want to go?"

"I'd love to. I tried to call, I wanted to thank you again for the fun time last night, when I couldn't raise anyone, I thought I'd drive out. It's a nice day, not too hot yet."

He tied Raven to the corral fence, and led the way to the other corral where the horse herd milled around. Jenny followed him inside the barn, smelling of dust and horse and old leather. Rand picked a halter off the wall, handed her a bridle and hefted the saddle unto his shoulder, motioning for Jenny to bring the saddle blanket.

He dropped the saddle near the fence, and caught Kid, who was gentle enough not to give him a token run around the corral. It didn't take Rand long to saddle the pinto, and Jenny held the halter rope and stroked the horse's nose, talking nonsense to him.

"You're such a pretty boy, and so nice. Oh, you like that," she said, stroking his bony face and scratching one fuzzy ear. She handed the lead over to Rand and he quickly exchanged the halter for the snaffle-bitted bridle, and handed the reins to Jenny.

"Here you go, lead him out of the corral before mounting," Rand opened the gate and shooed the other horses away while Jenny led Kid out.

As he was helping her mount, he noticed her wrists.

"What happened? That looks bad. I didn't notice that last night," He took her hand in his, turning it over to examine the scraped skin. His touch caused prickles of excitement to go through Jenny. She swallowed hard, not wanting to explain, yet at the same time wanting Rand to know about the latest dream.

"I told you about the dreams, and the one last night was the worse. Jen was tied up in an old shack, and her wrists got rubbed raw trying to loosen the ropes. Funny," she just noticed. "In the dream, her fingernails were broke, but mine are okay. That's weird."

Rand's face darken. "The whole thing is weird. I didn't think you were going back to Wild Rose."

Rand walked beside her back to where Raven was tied. The black horse whinnied happily as he saw his herd mate.

"He's glad to have company," Jenny said, smiling at Rand, trying to lighten the mood.

Rand wasn't charmed by her smile.

He mounted Raven and touched the horse with his spur. Jenny squeezed her legs to urge Kid into a trot to bring him up beside Raven.

"Tell me about the dream," Rand said.

She recounted the dream.

"I'm not sure if Wolf was killed or not," Jenny ended her recital. "Jen tried to throw off Molly's aim, I'm not sure if she was successful or not. Then I work up.

She wasn't sure what Rand's reaction would be, but she didn't expect anger.

"That's dangerous, Jenny. I don't want you going there. That town, those dreams, that's bad news. You've got to fight it." He looked out over the distance hills. The horses walked with a ground covering, easy stride.

"I want to find out what happened," Jenny said stubbornly. "Did

Wolf get killed? Who is Jen? Who was Molly? I'm getting closer to the end of the story. I have to find out. Aren't you curious too? Wolf was your great-great-grandfather.   Don't   you   care   what happened?"

"You're talking like this was a real historic event. How do you know that these dreams are based on real events?"

"All I know is that the people in them were real, well, Barney Morgan was, he was my great-great-grandfather. Wolf Logan was real, so was Sheriff Campbell and Jesse Arizona. Just because I haven't found anything to confirm the existence of Jen and Molly and Maria and Dr. Alex and 'Breed doesn't mean they weren't real. I suspect they were." She paused, then plunged forward. "I think Molly was Wolf's wife, and your great-great-grandmother."

"You're really serious about this, aren't you? Don't encourage it Jenny. I have a feeling it could be dangerous. Look at your wrists. What if this Jen gets killed, then what happens to you?"

"I'm more worried about what might happen to you if Wolf gets killed." Jenny admitted.

"Isn't that reason enough to quit?" Rand asked. "Maybe if you don't see it, it won't happen."

That was a new thought to Jenny. She was thinking if she knew it might happen, she could prevent it. Now, Rand said that maybe seeing the past would cause the future. Who was right? Could she avoid the possibility of Rand's being hurt by not dreaming? Could that have avoided Rand getting hurt when he got bucked off?

"I don't think I can get away from them until I learn what they are trying to tell me." Jenny laughed uneasily. "I don't want them to invade my house, I'd rather keep 'em in the ghost town. Unless

I give up the house and move back to Billings."

Rand pulled up Raven, reached over and grabbed Jenny's arm. "Look, I probably can't change your mind, and I don't want you to move away."

The admission made Jenny's heart take a wild leap.

She didn't say anything, and Rand continued. "But I know it's dangerous, and I know you can fight it." He paused. "I've never told anyone this, but I had the same experience once, and I fought it and won. I think. I've never actually have to nerve to test the theory."

"What happened?" Jenny asked. No wonder Rand believed her dreams.

They had dropped off the flats into a cedar-filled draw. It was cool in the draw, and a there was a tiny spring where the horses could water. Rand dismounted, let Raven water, and Jenny did the same with Kid. Then they tied the horses to a cedar and sat side by side on a rock outcropping.

Rand picked up a piece of a dead branch and began breaking it into smaller pieces.

"Well, one night, I think I was about 17, some some guys and I decided to camp out at Wolf's old homestead. I don't know why we choose that place, maybe because it was suppose to be haunted." He shrugged. "We were pretty cocky young bucks and I guess we wanted to prove we could..Typical high school seniors." He grinned at the memory. "We rode out, sleeping bags rolled up behind our saddles, and some smuggled beer wrapped up inside. We built a fire, and set around talking about, well, whatever. Then we banked the fire and went to sleep. I remember the dream....

1884

Wolf was riding his tall black

horse. The horse, anxious, was pulling at the bit, knowing home was just across the ridge. Topping the ridge, Wolf looked down. Where his cabin once stood was a still-smoking ruin. The sod walls still stood, but the roof had fallen in, the timbers burned and cracked.

Wolf slapped his spurs to the horse's sides, and horse fought for footing as he scrambled down the loose shale hillside. Then it buck-jumped into a gallop as they hit the flat-land.

Wolf pulled the horse up and was off and running to the cabin almost before Black Eagle skidded to a stop. Heedless of the still-smoldering ruins, Wolf began pulling at the timbers out, calling Molly's name.

Then he straighten, listened, and strode to the bushes near the creek. A heartbreaking sobbing was coming from the bushes. Wolf parted them to see Phelan, his dirty face streaked in tears, who threw out his arms and ran to his father, burying his face in Wolf's shoulders, hugging him in desperation and lonesomeness. "Pa, Pa."

Wolf hugged the boy for a long moment, then set him down and looked at him.

"Where's your ma,"

The boy shook his head, unable to speak.

"Was she in the cabin?" Again, the boy shook his head, tears running down his cheeks. He raised his arms again and Wolf picked him up. The boy snuggled into Wolf's shoulder.

His voice was muffled by Wolf's shirt. "A bunch of men, Pa. They rode in, and Ma told me to run and hide. But they wasn't interested in me. One man, he rode right up to Ma, then they went into the cabin. I don't know what happened. Then I saw the cabin burning."

"Listen, Little Wolf, had you ever

seen this man before?"

"Once. One time I was suppose to be in bed, and he came by. Ma talked to him for awhile, gave him coffee, then she saw me and sent me back to bed. Later, she came in told me to never tell nobody that he was here. She said if I did she would paddle me good. So I said I wouldn't tell. I'm sorry Pa," he wailed.

Wolf patted his back. "Its okay, son. I know. Can you tell me what the man looked like?"

"He was real tall, and wore big spurs. I could hear them jingling. He had red hair too,"

"Arizona." Wolf said.

"I found Mom's necklace. It fell down in the dirt as they rode away," the boy said, taking something out of his shirt.

Wolf took the necklace and curled it around his hand. He looked at for a long moment before shoving it into his shirt pocket. He put his hands on the boys shoulders and knelt down in front of him.

"Listen, Little Wolf, I have to go after the men who took your ma. You'll have to be brave and go live with Aunt Louella. She'll take care of you until I come back."

"Will Mommy be back?" The boy asked.

"I don't think so, Little Wolf. But I promise you I will be."

#########
PRESENT DAY

"I woke up then," Rand said. "The stars had moved a lot, the dipper was clear and distinct above us. I guess it was about two o'clock. The other guys were snoring. I could swear I smelled smoke, not just the smoke from the fire, the smell of burning wood and charred sod. It

306

smell different from the cedar wood we built the campfire with. I threw some more wood on the fire, and the rough bark rubbed my hands, and it seemed to hurt more than it should. I crawled back into the sleeping bag and drifted back to sleep. Then I had another dream.

1884

Two men, Wolf and short, dark haired man, were digging through the ruins of the cabin. The dark-haired man straightened and wiped the sweat from his round face.

"There's no body there, Wolf. Even in a fire like that, pieces of bone remain. There is no body here."

"Then what happened to my wife?" Wolf asked "Maybe they kidnapped her."

"Did you get anything demanding ransom?" the other man asked.

Wolf shook his head.

"No? Maybe they finished with her

and killed her later."

"Wouldn't Phelan have said something if they had taken her?"

The other man shrugged. "Maybe, maybe not. Maybe he didn't see anything, or maybe he blanked it out. The shock of seeing her ride away, seeing her abandoning him, could have been too much for his mind to handle."

"Phelan said Arizona had been there before, I wonder how many times?"

"Did she act frightened before all this happened? Do you think he threatened her?"

"No. In fact, she seemed pretty happy," Wolf said reflectively. "Almost too happy."

"You think she went with him willingly?"

"Maybe," Wolf said.

The other man shrugged. "I guess we'll never know, unless your boy decides to talk. But don't push him. He'll talk when he's ready."

"There's another way," Wolf said. "I can find Arizona."

#########

PRESENT DAY

"Then, it was morning. I was never so glad to see the sunrise as I was that morning. I never spent the night there again, and I didn't tell anyone else about the dreams, until now. Never had a reason too." Rand said. "The funny thing was, when I woke up, my hands were burned. I put wood on the fire, but I didn't touch the coals. The dreams were odd. On one level, I felt like a spectator, and on another I felt as if I were inside Wolf's head. Weird." He shook his head.

"Maybe yours weren't dreams either. Did it dawn on you that they might be telling both of us something? I want to find out what."

"Look, I tell you it's dangerous. But I'm not making any progress, am I?"

Jenny looked into his clear brown eyes, wondering if their budding relationship could stand her rebellion. But, she knew she couldn't give up the dreams. Not yet. She had to find the answers.

"So Molly must have been your great-great-grandmother. I'm are getting closer, Rand. Closer to the answers. I have to find out the rest of the story. I have to."

Rand stood up, held out his hand to help her, and walked back to the horses. In silence, they mounted and Jenny followed Rand as he rode off. They rode to the water hole. The recent heat wave had dropped the water-level, but there was a still an adequate amount for the cattle.

Rand hardly spoke at all on the ride back, except to point out a herd of pronghorn on the hillside and mule deer buck bedded down under a cut bank.

Back at the house, Jenny helped him unsaddle the horses, and watched as the horse herd trailed out the gate and back to pasture.

Rand offered her a drink of cold water, and she drank it quickly, then handed him back the glass. "I guess I'd better go," she said. "See you later,"

The phone rang and Rand answered it, and Jenny walked across the driveway back to her SUV, suddenly feeling the hollow feeling of loss. She drove under the Logan Longhorns sign and wondered if she would ever see Rand again. But, she couldn't give up the dreams.

It wasn't late when she got home. Even though she didn't feel like it, she recorded her dreams and Rand's dreams. She had fiction novel here. Maybe, once she got Barney's story finished, she would write a western novel using the characters and try to get it published.

Then, because it had been a short night and a depressing day, she slipped into a pair of shorts and a tank top and fell into bed for a nap. No dreams came, but when she woke it was nearly sunset. She felt the pull again.

Chapter 21
1885

Jen was sitting on the cabin floor, watching in horror as Wolf slowly crumbled to the floor, killed instantly with a bullet through the heart. Not far away, Jesse Arizona lay face-down on the floor, motionless.

Molly, now shocked by what she had done, dropped the pistol and began to cry. Jen was numb. She wanted to go to Wolf, wanted to breath life back into his body, but she couldn't move. She knew it was useless anyway. He was dead. Gone. Not shot by some outlaw in a fair fight, but gunned down by a woman he used to love.

She wondered if the shock of seeing Molly looking down the pistol barrel had caused him to hesitate long enough for Molly to get off the shot, or if Wolf's inherent sense of honor caused him to stay his hand, allowing Molly's bullet to find his mark. It didn't matter anyway. Jen picked up the discarded pistol and pointed it at Molly, but she couldn't pull the trigger. She couldn't kill anyone in cold blood. She lowered the pistol.

"You didn't have to shoot him," she said.

"He killed Jesse. I loved Jesse. He may have been a robber and a murder, but he loved me. He came by many times, always at night, always after the boy was

314

asleep."

"You ran off with him," Jen said. It wasn't a question. It was a statement of fact.

"Wolf was never there," Molly's voice rose. It whined in Jen's ear like a mosquito. "I was stuck in that cabin with a whining child. I begged Jesse to take me away, and finally he agreed. We planned the 'kidnapping' and I left Phelen. I knew that Wolf's family would care for him. I knew Jesse would persecute the boy because he was Wolf's. So I left him. Jesse just wanted me. He didn't want the boy."

"Now, you lost Jesse and you killed Wolf. Your scheming cost the lives of two men."

"It wasn't me," Molly said. "Wolf thought I was dead. He was chasing Jesse for his stage robberies. I told Jesse to quit, but he just laughed. Said he was smarter than any lawman. Now, Jesse's

315

dead and so is Wolf. It's fitting in a way."

Jen refused to look at the bodies. There was nothing to do now except to go back to Wild Rose, and hope that Judge Morgan was in town to arrest Campbell so he couldn't hide behind his badge to get rich off other illegal activities.

Jen rose from her seat on the floor. She wanted to take Molly in, but Molly had a gun as well, so Jen couldn't get the drop on her. She just hoped that Molly wouldn't shoot her.

Molly backed out the door, not taking her attention off Jen. "You won't shoot me in the back if I leave, will you?"

Jen shook her head wearily. "No. I won't shoot you. Go, Molly. If Judge Morgan wants you, he can seek you out. If you go far away, he might not find you." Molly actually didn't do anything illegal, and she would probably not be charged anyway. She could claim self-defense for the killing of Wolf.

Molly ran out of the cabin, and Jen heard her horse's hoof-beats fade into the distance. She was riding east, and Jen had to go west.

Jen walked over to Wolf's still body, and said her last goodbye. Then she walked out into the moonlit night, the faint light on the horizon told her that morning wasn't far off. She mounted Black Eagle, took the reins of Maria's horse, and rode away without a backward glance.

She couldn't bring Wolf back, but she could finish his work and bring a dishonest man to justice.

Chapter 22
Present

There were tears on Jenny's face when she woke, but overriding the sorrow was a feeling of panic. If the dreams were a warning, she had better heed it. Rand might be in danger. Even though they had parted on less than congenial terms yesterday, she had to find out, to make sure he was safe.

She started the Explorer, and headed toward the Logan ranch, driving as fast as she dared on the gravel road, the back end fishtailing once on the loose gravel when she had to hit the brakes to avoid hitting a mule deer and her spotted fawn.

Jenny's legs felt shaky after that and she slowed down, taking the next few miles at a slower pace.

When she bounced across the cattle guard under the Logan Longhorn sign, she saw an unfamiliar pickup near the house, and saw Rand's tall figure coming to the gate to see who the visitor was.

Jenny saw a man step out of the pickup, saw the deer rifle in his hand. He was so drunk he staggered and nearly fell against the pickup, but he kept his grip on the rifle, and leveled it at Rand. It was Keith Miller, who had accused Rand of taking Linda away from him, and who had been soundly thrashed by Dean on the day of the roping.

Jenny laid on the horn, and drove

straight at the man. He spun around, facing her. For a heart-stopping moment Jenny thought he might shoot her, but his nerve failed him and he jumped aside before she could run him down. She actually came close to hitting Rand but he leaped back out of the way and jumped on Keith before he could raise the rifle again. Rand twisted the gun from his hands and strong armed him into the house.

Keith was cursing and blustering, "You stole my woman, you polecat. She's got to be here somewhere, and I aim to find her."

"Call 911," Rand told Jenny as she followed them into the house. She dialed the number, gave the dispatcher the story, who said she would send the sheriff or a deputy down to arrest Keith.

Betty came in the back door, followed by Waylyn. Rand explained the situation to his parents, still holding the rifle on Keith.

Betty opened a draw and handed some clothesline rope to Waylyn, who tied Keith's hands securely. Jenny wished that Jesse Arizona had used that softer rope on her. Her wrists still burned.

Rand, now that Keith was securely tied, set the rifle in a corner of the kitchen. Keith began cursing Waylyn and Betty until Rand backhanded him across the mouth. "Don't you ever cuss in front of my mother, Miller. Or I'll put a bullet in that big mouth of yours."

Miller subsided with bad grace, but he shut up.

Rand looked at Jenny. "How did you happen to be here at the opportune moment? Isn't it a little early to come visiting?"

"Last night, in my dream, Wolf was shot and killed. I was so afraid that you might be in danger." In spite of how they

321

had parted yesterday, Jenny was so relieved that Rand wasn't injured that she spontaneously threw her arms around his neck and embraced him. Rand, after a startled moment, returned the embrace.

"Well, this time I guess I'm glad you had those dreams. Maybe that's why you were having them, and maybe you won't have any more."

Waylyn and Betty looked at them oddly.

Rand grinned. "Jenny has an interesting story to tell. We may as well hear it while we wait for the sheriff. Jenny, the floor is yours." Rand bowed and threw out a hand as if introducing her to an audience.

Jenny took a deep breath, telling them the short version of her dreams, and how she felt there was a reason for them, but she still had no idea what the reason was. Betty and Waylyn listened, occasionally asking questions or adding their own ideas.

They heard the county sheriff drive up. Rand met him in the driveway and told him what happened. He was a friend of the family, and greeted them cordially. "Attempted assault with a deadly weapon. He'll be in jail for some time on that,"

After he had taken Keith away, Betty said. "That was some story, Jenny. You know, there's a trunk up in the attic. It's been locked since I can remember. It was Phelan's. Maybe there's something in there about Wolf."

"I remember Rand saying something about that one day," Jenny said. "I guess we both forgot."

Rand led Jenny into the attic, which was dusty but tidy. Rand sent the flashlight beam across the floor, and found the humpbacked trunk.

"Let's take it downstairs, where there's more light." Each taking a handle, they got the truck down the stairs, and set it on the back porch.

Betty arrived with a dust cloth. "Wipe it off, first," she said.

Inside was a confusion of papers, books, and just plain junk. An old pistol, with the initials WL carved in the stock, and a pair of large roweled spurs. Jenny touched the pistol and felt a chill. Rand looked pale. It was Wolf's own gun. Jenny remembered the spurs on Wolf's boots when he walked across the floor of her small house.

Jenny found a lumpy envelope addressed to Phelan Logan. Postmarked 1910. There was no return address. Jenny handed it to Rand, who opened if as gingerly as if he were afraid there was a rattlesnake inside, but there were only two small objects and a note, brittle with age. "These were your mother's. I thought you might want them." The letter wasn't signed. The objects were the turquoise earrings that matched Jenny's necklace. The tiny howling wolves were almost lifelike, and they seemed to glow.

"Molly's earrings. She must have sent them to Phelan."

"More likely someone else sent them after she died." Rand said, turning the earrings over in his hand. "So my great-great-grandmother was an outlaw. I wonder what she did after her lover was killed."

"It's hard to tell. But now I'm sure she was Wolf's first wife. I wonder why she ran off with Jesse?"

"I doubt that we'll ever know," Rand said. "At least, I'm content to let it rest. How about you?"

Jenny argued with herself, then decided that she didn't want any untruthfulness between them. "I want to go back, Rand, I'm sure the worst is over, and I want to find out now what happened to Jen," Jenny told him.

"My   great-great-grandmother, Kathy, lived to be over 100, and raised two boys. One never married. My grandfather only had one child, my father. Kathy left a request in her will that the first girl-child would be named Jennifer. I was the first, I inherited the name. I think Jen Carlise and Kathy Sanders were the same person, my great-great-grandmother, and I think she named me Jenny to carry on her name."

Rand sighed. "Okay, Jenny. I know enough not to argue with a bull headed woman. Go ahead. Like you said, the worst is probably over." He leaned over and kissed her. "That night at the dance, was it Wolf you were thinking of? I felt there was somebody. Funny, I'm guess I was   jealous   of   my   great-great-grandfather. That is really weird."

"Yes. I couldn't explain it to you then, but I kept getting flashes of Wolf and Jen that night. On one level I guess

I'm in love with him, but it is almost the same as being in love with you."

"I guess," Rand said, and Jenny hoped she hadn't shown her hand too quickly.

Betty and Waylyn were astonished at the discovery, and how Jenny's dreams seemed to tie everything together.

When Jenny showed them the necklace, Betty and Waylyn agreed with Rand that Jenny should have the earrings, but she declined. "These belong to your family. They were given to Phelan, like Wolf gave the necklace to Jen."

Rand didn't argue with her, instead he put the earrings in his shirt pocket.

"I'd better get home," Jen said. "It has been a wild morning and I, well, I didn't sleep too well last night. I need to go home and unwind."

Rand walked her to the Explorer. After she got in he leaned in the window.

"Thanks, Jenny. If you hadn't

arrived in the nick of time, that damn fool might have shot me. I guess those dreams are good for something. But, take care of yourself. Anyway, I guess I'm kind of curious too, so let me know what else you find out."

Rand went back to the house and Jenny started the Explorer and turned out of the driveway. Back home, she typed her latest dream into the computer. She was sure that Jen became Kathy Sanders, but she wasn't sure how or why or who she really was. Maybe she could find something more in the old newspapers.

Gathering up her pens and paper, she drove to Red Bluffs. She asked the librarian if she could use the microfiche machine, after assuring her she knew how to use it, and she found the newspapers from the years 1885 and 1886.

It took her quite a while to find the story, and then it was so short that Jenny felt more frustrated than ever. All it said was that Sheriff Campbell, a part of the Arizona gang, had been, "*Relieved of his duties as sheriff and sentenced to 'hang by the neck' until dead.*" The sentence was passed down by Barney Morgan, but there was no mention of Wolf or Jen.

A few weeks later in the paper she found a small notice in the legal notices, or whatever they called them back then, marriage license issued to Barney T. Morgan and Kathy L. Sanders," That was it, no mention of parents or when the ceremony was to be. She already had a copy of the marriage license, and it told her nothing. After she turned off the machine and returned the microfiche to the drawer, she saw the shadows were laying long on the lawn outside the window. It was evening; the expectant humming was beginning to run through her body.

#######
1886

The stage coach waited, and two people were getting off, Barney Morgan and Jen. They walked into the registry office, and signed their names to the marriage license. This was same the marriage license that Jenny had copied in the courthouse.

Then she could hear Jen speaking. "Kathy was my grandmother's name, and Sanders was my mother's maiden name. No one could connect me with Jen Carlise , Wolf Logan's woman."

"I wouldn't care," Barney said. "Wolf was a good man, and my friend. Without him, and you, Campbell would still be at large. To protect you, the woman Wolf loved, gives me great honor. You can keep your name, Jen.

"You will be a great man in the

territory someday," Jen said. "You won't need the press to condemn you because of you're wife's past. It is better this way. I am a new person. Jen died that night with Wolf. Kathy Sanders rose from the Phoenix's ashes."

"Whatever you say, Kathy Sanders," Barney said, pushing the marriage license across the counter. "The judge is waiting to marry us, shall we go?"

#######

Jenny woke briefly, stretched, flipped on the key and looked at the dashboard clock. "3 am." Jenny muttered, then she turned off the key, squirmed around to get more comfortable, and fell back asleep.

#######
1886

Jen and Barney were sitting at Jen's kitchen table, arguing. "You don't have to testify." Barney was saying. "I have enough against Campbell anyway."

"I want to testify," Jen said "Its what Wolf would have wanted. Indirectly, Campbell was responsible for Wolf's death, I want to make sure he pays for that." Jen took a deep breath. "Also, the people in Wild Rose only knew Wolf was a bounty hunter, and looked down on him for that. They thought he killed for money, but money wasn't the reason, was it?"

"No. Wolf had a strong sense of justice, and he preferred to bring them to trial when he could. When he began chasing Arizona and Campbell, he saw how the corrupt the law could be if in the wrong hands, and he began to bring them in across the saddle more often. Many times they drew first, but you know Wolf, and I believe sometimes he goaded them into drawing first."

"Also, Molly ran off with Arizona and abandoned his son. That gnawed at him, and preyed on his mind after that," Jen said thoughtfully.

"We all have our faults, and our weaknesses. Arizona was Wolf's."

Jen nodded. "I want the people in Wild Rose to know that he was working for the law, not against it. I guess I want justice from them as well."

"It's too bad," Barney said, running his hand across the table in Jen's house. "Wolf was a good man, he would have been an excellent sheriff. I offered to help him if he wanted to run, but he didn't want to be held to the law. If he found Arizona, he wanted justice, and wanted to do whatever it took to administer that justice."

"That's why I want to testify," Jen said.

Barney sighed. "OK. Come to the trial, I'll let the prosecutor know you're there, but to only call on you if he feels your testimony will sway the jury. Agreed?"

Jen nodded. "Agreed."

The court room was crowded with men. Only a few women were sprinkled through the crowd. The jurors were all men.

Barney Morgan, in his black robes, sat on bench, an angry look on his face, as he listened to the long-winded testimony of the man on the witness stand.

Causing almost no stir among the spectators, a lone woman, dressed in black with a black veil covering her face, slipped in the doors and into a seat near the back of the courtroom.

Barney's eyes flicked over her

briefly. He and the prosecutor exchanged a silent message.

Sheriff Campbell was sitting near the bench, looking smug. The long winded defense council was rambling, extorting the virtues of Sheriff Campbell and the absurdity of the charges being brought against him.

"The prosecution wants you to believe that our good Sheriff Campbell was in league with Jesse Arizona, and how he would tell the gang which stages to rob. Plus, they want you to believe that Sheriff Campbell twice aided and abetted Arizona's escapes from his jail each time he was caught. Isn't it possible that Arizona was simply a hard man to hold?" He looked at the jury, gauging their reaction. Most seemed unimpressed, Jen thought.

"Could he not have arranged with his gang to help him escape? I'm sure every sheriff in the West has had some prisoners escape, Campbell had no knowledge of Arizona's escapes until after they happened. To say that our good sheriff 'allowed' him to escape is laughable."

He paused. "Gentlemen of the jury, this man has spend five years of his life here in Wild Rose, bringing law and order to the area. Please don't let some wild accusations of these people rob the man of his life's work, and possibly, his life.

"All in all," the defense was saying, "Campbell has been a great sheriff for our town."

"Step down please," Barney said. "Prosecution, call your next witness."

"The prosecution calls Miss Jenny Morgan ."

A mutter ran through the crowd, and Sheriff Campbell, Jen was glad to see, suddenly looked pale, and sweat beaded his forehead. He was afraid, and

Jen was glad of it. Barney Morgan leaned back in his chair and smiled.

Jen stated her name and place of residence, Wild Rose. Her voice carried through the entire courtroom as she looked the man with the Bible square in the eye and said, "I do."

She was prepared to tell the truth, and she told her story, starting from the night that Wolf was wounded, seeing Arizona and Campbell together, and relating the conversations between Arizona and Breed. She left out Molly, knowing that she had no bearing on the case.

Then, it was over. The defense asked her a few questions, but it was obvious to Jen that her testimony had swung the scales of justice. The jury only deliberated an hour before the court reconvened and Barney pronounced the sentence on Sheriff Campbell.

Barney Morgan, sans robes, met Jen

waiting on the seat of the buggy.

"It's done," Jen said.

"Well done, my love," Barney said, taking up the reins and chirping to the horses, who broke into a walk then a trot as he flipped the reins against their rumps. "Wolf would have been proud."

Jen turned in the seat to take a last look at her small house. Her belongings were stowed in the back of the buggy, and this would be her last day living in the town she had loved.

Even though it would be their shopping center for a time, she would now live with her husband on his homestead, and follow him wherever his aspirations led him. Also in the back of the buggy, waving a little in the breeze, was a pot of red poppies, and a pot of wild rose starts, which Marie gave Jen from her garden.

"We will have a good life, Kathy," Barney said.

"Yes, my love, we will," Kathy said, and turned her eyes forward, looking into the future instead of back at the past.

Chapter 23
Present

Jenny woke from the dream. The ruins were ruins again, and she knew the dreams had ended. She had the answers. Kathy Sanders and Jen Morgan were the same person. Jen was her great-great-grandmother, and Wolf's lover.

Back at her house, she saw Rand's pickup, and Rand resting his arms on the side of the bed. He turned as she drove up.

"I was getting ready to come to the ghost town to look for you," he said. "I am glad to see you are in one piece. Did you find the answers you seek?" He grinned.

"I did. Jen was Kathy Sanders, she changed her name so that there would be no connect between Jen Carlise, Wolf's consort, and Kathy Sanders, the wife of a judge, later to be a senator. She didn't want anything to hurt her new husband's career. That was why my great-great-grandmother named me Jenny. She wanted some part of her past life to survive."

"Do you think the dreams are over?"

"I'm sure they are. They were telling me what I needed to know, and now Wild Rose, Jen and Wolf can rest in peace." She searched Rand's handsome face. "I think the dreams tried to tell me something else, too."

Rand held up his hand. "I feel it too. You think that you and I are Wolf and Jen, reincarnated or something like that. Being a skeptical person, I won't point out the reasons against such a claim, I'll believe it if you do."

He took her in his arms and kissed her thoroughly, sweetly. "I suspect you believe their ghosts have been waiting here all along, just waiting for you come here and we could finish their story, right?"

Jenny laughed. "Right." She raised her lips back to his, and he kissed her again. Only once did Wolf overshadow Rand, then he was gone. Jenny knew, with a mixture of relief and sadness, that she would never see his dark, rough-hew features again.

Rand reached into his shirt pocket and pulled out the earrings. "These are sort of my pre-engagement promise. I've thought about it all summer, and I want to marry you, Jenny, weird dreams and all. If you can stop thinking about Wolf long enough to think about me. That's why I didn't want you to go back to Billings. What about it?"

Jenny looked at the earrings that Rand had dropped into her hand. Wolf and Jen, Rand and Jenny. It was meant to be, somewhere in the vast reaches of time.

"Oh, Rand, yes. Of course. And, I have a feeling that Wolf is where he belongs again, in the past. I'm content to leave him there."

Rand opened his arms and Jenny stepped into his embrace. It was Rand. There was no overshadowing of Wolf Logan.   Just Rand's warmth, Rand's embrace.

"You are going to invite me in, aren't you," Rand whispered, his breath stirring the hair by her ear.

Jenny laughed, and led the way

into the house.

"I'm going to see if the owner will sell me this house," Jenny said as she led Rand into the bedroom. "I think it was Jen's house, and it's kind of growing on me."

"No problem," Rand said. "I can put in a good word for you. The realtor who owns it is my aunt."

"Thanks," Jenny said.

"But why buy it? We can live out on the ranch, in my house. It's a nice house, we just put it up eight years ago."

"I know, but I still want it. Just because it was Jen's. So what if we don't live here full time, I still want it. Maybe I can convert it into a writing studio or something. After I finish Barney's book, I'm going to write a western novel."

"About Wolf?"

"Yes, Wolf and Jen. If your family doesn't mind."

"I think it would make a great

book. But, right now, let's put Wolf and Jen to rest, I don't want them looking over my shoulder." Then he flopped down on the bed and pulled Jenny down beside him, kissing her cheek and her neck.

The chapter on Wolf Logan was closed. Now, it was just Rand and Jenny. Jenny felt like Jen and Wolf were watching them, and would have approved.

But she didn't tell Rand.

EPILOG

Jenny's book came out the next year. It had been an exciting year, partly the book but mostly Rand. They had dated for a few months, then planned a lovely wedding in Crystal Creek, at Rand's church.

After Jenny finished Barney's story, she began work on a western novel, using Wolf as the main character.

There was a reception for Jenny's book held in the Governor's mansion in Cheyenne, Wyoming. Jenny and Rand attended, planning to go to Denver for their honeymoon afterward.

The mansion was as elaborate as Jenny had imagined, but she hadn't expected to see an antique candelabra sitting on a small table in the hall. The brass plate under the candelabra said it had been presented to the Governor of Wyoming Territory in 1885.

"Rand, look," Jenny said, pulling Rand over to the table. "It has to be the same one that Wolf and Barney talked about in my dream. It has to be." More proof of how accurate the dreams had been. She was already thinking of a way to work it into her novel.

"Pretty cool," Rand said. "Wolf helped to save this from the outlaws, and it's where it belongs."

Rand was right. The candelabra was where it belonged. She touched the blue stones of the turquoise necklace, and felt the earrings brush her neck.

They, too, were where they belonged.

And, tonight, at the hotel in Denver, she would be where she belonged, in Rand's arms.

About the Author

Cynthia Vannoy has published ten books, on subjects ranging from martial arts to taxidermy. She is interested in the paranormal and enjoyed writing about it in Blue Turquoise.

She mostly enjoys writing about her home state, Wyoming, where she still lives on the family ranch that was started by her grandfather. She enjoys listening to the birds, working outside and riding her horses, Sugar Bear and Brown Raven.

Blue Turquoise   Vannoy

www.ingramcontent.com/pod-product-compliance
Lightning Source LLC
Chambersburg PA
CBHW071847220626
47052CB00002B/10